THE Jackets

LIZ DEJESUS

Arte Público Press
Houston, Texas

The Jackets is made possible through grants from the City of Houston through the Houston Arts Alliance.

Recovering the past, creating the future

Arte Público Press
University of Houston
452 Cullen Performance Hall
Houston, Texas 77204-2004

Cover design by Mora Des!gn

DeJesus, Liz
    The Jackets / by Liz DeJesus.
        p.   cm.
    ISBN 978-155885-603-5 (alk. paper)
    1. Love stories, American. I. Title.
PS3604.E35J33 2011
813′.54—dc22

                                                    2010054264
                                                          CIP

∞ The paper used in this publication meets the requirements of the American National Standard for Information Sciences—Permanence of Paper for Printed Library Materials, ANSI Z39.48-1984.

11 12 13 14 15 16 17   10 9 8 7 6 5 4 3 2 1

To Kurt,
te amo, mi amor

Acknowledgments

Thanks first and foremost to God for listening to my prayers and answering them. I never could've imagined any of this for myself.

I want to thank my husband Kurt, I know it isn't easy being around someone that's constantly living inside her head so thank you for your love and patience. I also wish to thank my family and my friends who have stood by me through thick and thin.

Mason, my little boy . . . the little star of my life. Every day with you is amazing. I love you so much.

Red

She was a spot of red that could be seen from miles away. Like a blood-red cardinal flying above an ocean of grey. The sky, the sidewalks, the streets, even the cars. Laura stood out as she walked slowly, steadily from her house to her job at the paper store. The cold wind blew across her face like cold knives slicing across her skin. She pulled her cherry jacket tighter against her body. Her short brown hair became a tornado on top of her head.

People couldn't help but stare. Laura's face remained stagnant, but out of the corner of her eyes she could see men pressing their faces against the windshield of their cars to get a better look at her. She was a flash of color in the middle of all that colorless muck. She hadn't really planned on wearing that jacket that day or the days that followed. It was the first thing she grabbed from her closet. Then again, everything in her closet had color. Sapphire. Amethyst. Moss. Fire. Sunflower. Crimson. Colors she loved more than life itself. That was all she ever cared about . . . color. It was the only thing she ever wanted to talk about.

"Why are they staring?" Laura wondered as she shook her head in confusion. "It's just a red jacket."

Allen was in the kitchen, trying to stay awake so he could get to work alive and get the day over with. He couldn't start the day without a cup of coffee. He muttered to himself as he moved around the kitchen. He glanced out the window and sighed. He thought about all the things that needed to get done at the office. He took a sip and made a face.

"Ugh." He pulled the cup away from his body like it was something that meant to do him harm.

He brewed fresh coffee and poured a cup, spilling some on his hand. He pulled it away and tried to shake off the burning feeling.

Stupid, friggin' . . .

Allen looked up and stopped everything. Red. He couldn't help but stare. He couldn't turn and look the other way. His dark blue eyes stayed on her. He didn't understand why the blood that ran through his veins had suddenly caught fire.

She's a rose trying to bloom in the middle of a storm.

"Where's she going?" he asked himself. Allen made it his morning habit to stand in front of his kitchen window and watch "The Woman in Red" walk by as he drank his coffee. Allen didn't want to call her "The Girl" or anything silly like that because she most certainly wasn't a girl.

Every morning, Allen waited for her to appear. She was always punctual. At eight-thirty without fail she would walk past his house. It was one of the few things in this world he could count on. Saturdays and Sundays were the only two days he didn't see her.

One day, she didn't appear. At first he thought that maybe she was late.

Maybe . . . she's sick.

He took a sip of his coffee, and already it didn't taste the same. For some reason, seeing her made it a little easier to swallow the watery tar he called coffee in the mornings. Allen didn't know why he persisted on making it.

I should stop buying the dollar store brand.

He poured it all down the sink and made up his mind to buy the more expensive brand the next time he went grocery shopping. He watched as the brown liquid swirled down the drain, until it was no more. He waited. Allen looked for her like a man lost at sea seeking a sandy shore. She had never been late before. Even on rainy days she was on time. Always.

Why go crazy over a woman who I don't even know?

He looked again and saw a woman who reminded him of her.

It can't be her . . . she's not wearing her red jacket.

He took a closer look and saw that it *was* the same woman. Only she lacked the ghost of a smile that was always on her lips. Her skin was pale and her eyes were sunken.

What happened? Where did the color go? Her fire?

Her eyes were as black as coal.

Laura felt someone looking at her. She saw no one. She looked to her right and found herself staring into a pair of haunting blue eyes. Laura smiled, waved and kept walking.

Yesterday sucked.

"Thanks for stopping by, have a nice day," Laura said as she handed Mrs. Ling her bag.

"Bye, bye." Mrs. Ling took leave.

Mrs. Ling was a nice Chinese lady who could say only a handful of phrases. She was so old her face looked like a mountain in Sedona. Her eyes were barely there, just slits with lashes. Seeing her always put a smile on Laura's face.

As Mrs. Ling walked out of the store, Laura began putting stacks of paper away, when she heard the bell above the door ring.

"I'll be with you in just one second," she called out over her shoulder.

"Don't worry. I can wait."

The voice sent chills down her spine. *Why was he here?*

"Hi, Steve." She tried to hide the displeasure in her voice. The last thing she wanted to do was cause a scene at work.

"Can we talk?" he asked.

"Not now." Laura smiled.

"Don't give me that."

"Remember the last time when we tried to talk? Besides, I'm busy. I have work to do and customers."

"Just five minutes."

"I really don't want to do this now." Laura searched the store for someone bigger than him and found no one.

"Fucking talk to me!" Steve yelled, knocking down a shelf of stationary.

Scores of pastel paper fell on the floor in colorful waves. It was beautiful and sad all at once.

All eyes were on Laura.

"You're going to have to get out of here, young man," ordered Jim, the manager, from behind her.

Steve could definitely take Jim if he wanted, but he knew Jim could call the cops and show them the store videotape. Steve wasn't completely stupid. He turned and marched out of the store without saying anything else.

"I'm so sorry," Laura muttered, embarrassed. "I'll clean this all up." She quickly fell to her knees and started to tidy up.

"Laura, I think you should go, too," Jim said.

"Jim . . . please." She couldn't even hold her head up to look at him.

"I'm sorry. But I can't keep cleaning up the mess that jerk leaves behind."

Laura cried all the way home. *Please, God . . . something good. A little bit of luck is all I need.*

The Jackets

Laura looked into the house once more and saw that the man with the large blue eyes was still standing there.

A smile. That was all he needed. It was the sign he was waiting for. Allen ran outside and caught up to her. He would be late for work, but he didn't care. It was one of those now-or-never moments. He had thirty seconds to come up with something witty to say to her. Something that would make her listen to him.

"What happened?" he asked.

Laura put her hands up, frightened by Allen's sudden appearance. She looked into his eyes and realized that it was the man with the haunting eyes. She put her hands down slowly.

"What are you talking about?" she asked.

"Your red jacket . . . "

"My jacket?" She looked at him, confused.

Her lips mouthed an "Oh" as she realized that he was talking about her favorite red jacket. There was plenty of history in that little bit of cloth. She had it on when she had her first kiss. First job interview. First day at work. It was a jacket she wore on days she knew would be filled with firsts. Every time she wore that blood-red jacket, her world was brighter, filled with possibilities, almost as if anything could happen.

She balanced herself on her heels for a moment and looked at the sky as she gave Allen her response. "It was time to grow up, I guess." She shrugged and put her hands in her pockets.

"No," Allen whispered.

He shook his head.

"It's just a jacket," Laura said.

It became clear to Allen that she didn't see the world as he did. Did she not see the grey that enveloped her?

"What's your name?" she asked.

"Allen Foster."

"Nice to meet you, Allen. I'm Laura Reyes," she said and extended her hand to him.

Allen took her hand and marveled over how well it slipped into his, as if a piece of a puzzle had just been handed to him. He held her hand for a second longer than he should have. Her hand was soft and smooth.

"So, why were you so concerned over my not wearing my red jacket today?"

She studied his face as he thought of an answer. He had a kind face. He wasn't terribly handsome, but there was something about him that made her feel warm inside. She realized that it was his smile. He had a wide, easy smile.

"Because . . . the thought of this world draining the color out of you was sad," Allen finally said. "I was ready to mourn the loss of anything interesting ever happening in my life, and then you walked by my house as though nothing could touch you. As though nothing could possibly affect you. Because seeing you in the mornings gave me hope. It made the day . . . bearable. You gave me something to look forward to every morning."

"I see," she said.

Lightning danced across the sky. Thunder rolled above them, bringing the promise of rain along with it. Laura looked up and sighed.

Allen admired her long neck. He couldn't believe he was talking to her. He wanted to touch her. He wanted to reassure himself that she was real. He wanted to take away everything in her that was sad and set it on fire. To watch it burn into a pile of ashes.

Laura looked into Allen's eyes and said, "The world has moments that make most of us despair over what tomorrow will bring. You just have to learn how to carry bits of color within yourself. Not let others carry them for you."

The Jackets

Laura pointed at her feet. Allen looked down to see a pair of tiny pointed shoes peeking through her indigo jean pants. They were red.

Allen chuckled. He knew that from this moment on he wanted to have her with him always.

Laura loved how his sandy-blonde hair glinted with help from the little bit of sunlight that managed to break through the clouds, how his blue eyes sparkled. If anything, he was much more colorful than she.

"Would you like to have a cup of coffee with me?" he asked.

"I guess I can risk that much for a handsome stranger."

Allen offered her his hand, which Laura took and walked away with him.

Orange

ia wasn't *on* fire. She *was* fire. Not the kind of flame that consumes, leaving nothing but smoke or ashes. Mia was more like the fire used to keep a body warm on a cold winter night. The torch used to guide the lost out of the darkness. She was warmth, or at least everything I thought warmth should be. But that's not good enough for some people. Some people prefer the cold darkness found on a starless night. For some reason these were the people that Mia was always reaching out to, her ivory hands trying to break through the barriers they put around themselves. Sometimes it was worthwhile and other times it was just a waste of time. I know because I was one of those people she reached out to.

I'll never forget the night I saw her for the first time. I had had another argument with my then-girlfriend Mallory right in the middle of a party, and instead of dealing with it, I walked out of the room. I remember trying to light my cigarette, but my lighter wasn't working. All I was getting from the damned thing were sparks and bits of smoke. I must've been swearing or more likely making a smart-ass comment about the lighter because Mia giggled as she struck a match and held it before my cigarette.

She didn't say a word. Just held the match long enough for the tip of my cigarette to glow, our eyes staring intently into each other. The light from the match gave her face a soft glow. Her brown eyes were beckoning orbs. I couldn't pull myself away from them. They made me feel like I was more than just another person standing out in the cold, struggling with a bad lighter. Mia made me feel warm—even for that one instant. Before I could say "Thank you," she walked away.

I broke up with Mallory that night. Best decision I ever made in my whole friggin' life. Mallory had done everything in her power to belittle me.

Fast forward into the future a couple of months, and here I am at Jake's party . . . only . . . alone. Since that fateful night, I've seen Mia a handful of times. Not really enough to get to know her. All I can do is practice my voyeuristic tendencies whenever she's around. In other words, I haven't had the guts to ask her out on a date. God . . . why am I such a wimp?

And here I am, chatting with Mia and Jake.

"Do you shave your pubes?" Jake asks.

Screeching tires in the back of my mind draw all thoughts to a halt. Well . . . he certainly got my attention. This is how I know Jake is drunk, but my jaw drops anyway. I look at Mia to see her reaction. She's calmly sipping her soda, all the while keeping her eyes on Jake.

Finally, she calmly pulls the glass away from her lips, smiles and in a dead-serious voice answers, "That's a personal question."

"I just wanna know what I have to do to get Danielle to do it," Jake says.

Jake, I think to myself, *stop talking.* But it's like watching a man sink in quicksand while he's playing a video game. He doesn't know what's happening around him. He doesn't know that he's going to die a slow and painful death unless someone swoops in and rescues him.

The Jackets

I wasn't going to save him, not this time.

"It's a woman's choice whether or not she wants to. Just because you see it in a porno doesn't mean that every girl does it."

"So you're saying *you* don't shave," Jake slurs.

"You're a fucking dick." Mia rolls her eyes.

"Do you at least trim?"

"Jesus Christ, Jake. I can't believe you're asking that," I finally blurt out.

"It's okay, Evan. I can handle this one." Mia winks at me. "Jake, to answer your question . . . no, I don't shave. I don't like having to stop every five steps to scratch my crotch. And yes, in the summer-time I do trim. But only because I don't feel like walking around the beach as though I were smuggling Chewbacca's love child between my thighs.

"And you're lucky Danielle will at least touch your dick. So shut the fuck up and enjoy the fact that there's still a woman out there that lets you kiss her."

She . . . rocks. I laugh and then cover my mouth. I'm not sure if it's okay for me to. I can't believe she's said all of that. I've never heard a woman talk to a man that way before. Jake totally deserved it. He's a numb-nuts.

Mia catches me staring at her, and I quickly turn from her dark-brown eyes as I feel myself turning bright red. I peek in her direction and notice her smirk and turn away. I let out a sigh of relief. I don't know what I'd do if she ever finds out how I really feel about her.

"All right, people, I'm gonna go now," Mia announces. "I think I've had enough excitement for one night. Plus, I have to go to work early tomorrow morning."

You know you're liked when everyone in the room protests when you say you're leaving. No one ever does that for me. Most of the time people just say "Bye!"

"What are you gonna do at home? Stay here. Don't let my idiot brother drive you away," Laura tells her.

Laura and I dated for a while a few years ago. Lucky for us we realized how wrong we were for each other and stayed friends. One less woman that wants to put my balls in a pickle jar.

"How're you going to get home anyway? Isn't your car at the mechanic's?" Penelope asks.

"I'll take the bus. It runs until midnight," Mia says as she puts her pumpkin-colored corduroy jacket on and wraps a moss-green scarf around her neck.

"You're not going to actually stand at the bus stop in this cold weather?" Laura asks as she looks out the window.

"It's not that bad, once you get used to the numb feeling your fingers get after standing there for half an hour," Mia jokes, putting her red gloves on.

"Evan, you, asshole, don't just sit there. Give Mia a ride. She doesn't live that far from your house," Laura says.

"H-Huh? W-What?" I stutter.

Oh shit, my big opportunity. I can't breathe. Breathe, you asshole! Breathe!

"What do you say? Care to avoid me doing my human Popsicle impersonation?" Mia grins.

I turn to Jake, and he mouths the word "Go" at me while rolling his eyes toward the front door. I smile at my chance. I start to breathe again.

"All right, let me go get my coat and keys," I say, not wasting another second.

"Sweet," Mia rejoices, clapping her hands together excitedly. *Why does she have to be so cute?*

We're in my car. She smells great. Like flowers . . . or something that comes from a nice bottle with girly stuff in it. I've never been this close to her before. I don't think I've ever been more nervous in my entire life. Good thing all I'm doing is taking her home. I turn and smile at her. She grins and thanks me for giving her a ride home. I nod and turn my eyes back on the road. No sense getting us both killed because I'm stupid in love with the most beautiful girl I've ever seen. God, what kind of an idiot am I?

"You're welcome." *That's not so hard. Two words.*

I always have a version of what I want to do rolling in the back of my head. Well, I have tons of scenarios, except I have them set up in how many ways it could go wrong. Sure, I'm taking her home, but what if I start talking and get comfortable around her, and then we get into a car accident, and then she decides to never get in a car with me . . . ever again. What if I turn on the radio and a song she hates pops up and ruins the mood I could've created? Or worse, a song that some evil ex-boyfriend dedicated to her pops up and makes her cry? Too many scenarios. I have hundreds of these things. It sickens the mind at times, especially mine.

"So . . . ," Mia starts to say as I take the ramp to I-95.

"So . . . ," I echo.

So? So? What kind of dumb-ass thing is that to say to someone? I want to pull my own hair out in the most painful way possible. *I'm in love with you! I want to have lots of sex with you! In my house! On my bed! On the kitchen floor! In this car! Actually, in the backseat of this car would be nice.* That's what I should've said, not . . . *So.* I don't deserve to live.

"What's new with you, Evan?"

"Not much. You can turn the radio on if you want to," I say, gripping the steering wheel and watching my hands turn white.

Yes, something's new with me. More and more fantasies of you pop up in my mind each and every day. But I can't say that because that's just wrong.

"I don't believe that," she replies.

"Huh? Why not?"

"Do you brush your teeth the same way every day?"

I actually take a moment to think about that. "No."

"Do you take a piss the same way every day?"

My mouth hangs open for the second time tonight. I can't believe she's asked such a blunt question. She's completely shattering the illusion I have of her being this delicate, fragile young woman. But I don't mind it at all . . . not one bit.

"Umm. I dunno."

"Well then, how do you know something new didn't happen to you today?"

"I guess, you're right," I agree.

"So, come on, tell me about your day. . . . " She has this look on her face as though she's won some sort of argument I didn't know we were having.

"I woke up this morning with a headache. That happens to me whenever it's going to rain or snow. So I figured one or the other was going to happen today. I took a few aspirins. And I had eggs and bacon for breakfast."

I don't mention that I masturbated three times and went to the video store to buy some porn. These are things she really doesn't need to know. I glance over real quick to see if she's bored with my story, but I see that I have her full attention.

"Also . . . I didn't really feel like coming to Jake's party."

"How come?"

"Besides the fact that he loves being a dick to you for some reason, I hate when you leave," I confess.

"Oh . . . "

We drive in silence for a few minutes, then I see the first few flakes of snow dance across my windshield. She leans over, turns on the radio and searches for a song. She must have super hearing because all I can hear is two-point-two seconds of something and then static. When she stops fiddling with the radio, I'm amazed at her choice of music. It's "Somebody to Love" by Queen. She sings along and even though her voice is not Freddy Mercury's, she isn't that bad. I stay quiet until the song is finished. I'm enjoying her company so much, I don't want to ruin the moment by talking. The chances of me saying something stupid are just too high.

"Isn't Queen friggin' awesome?" she asks after the song ends.

I nod in agreement.

"It's starting to snow. I can't believe you were going to stand out in this cold weather wearing nothing but that little jacket of yours."

"It's warmer than you think." She pulls the burnt orange jacket closer to her body.

"If you say so."

"Take this next exit."

"Okay." I notice that the snow has started to fall much faster.

I ask Mia to find a station that's covering the weather. And according to the news, we're driving in the middle of a snowstorm.

"Well . . . shit," she says.

"That sums it up nicely." I turn on the windshield wipers.

"Lucky for us we're not that far from my place."

"Cool."

She continues to give me directions until we reach her house. I stop the car. We sit there in silence, the engine running, watching the snow lightly skating across the hood. I don't know what to say. Apparently neither does Mia. The windshield wipers swish softly left and right, pushing the oncoming snow away from the glass.

"This is fucking dumb," Mia blurts out.

"What is?"

"I'm not going to let you drive back home in the middle of a snow storm. I won't be able to sleep tonight. Look at the size of those snowflakes. They're the size of my thumb!"

"I could always sleep in the car, if it makes you feel better," I mutter.

"No, you silly ass. You can come inside and sleep on my couch. I'm sure I have a pair of pajama bottoms you can use."

"Won't your boyfriend mind?"

I figure it's was a valid question until I notice how she's staring at me like I'm from another planet. What the hell do I know? This is the first time I've said more than ten words to her, and muttering doesn't count.

All of a sudden, she's laughing like it was the funniest thing she's ever heard in her life. I need a gun. Or at least something that can give me a quick and painless death.

"That's funny. Me, have a boyfriend. . . . "

"So, no boyfriend?"

"Not with the extra twenty pounds I have on this body, I won't," she says as she pinches a little bit of skin on her belly.

"Are you kidding me?"

"No guy wants a fatty."

She pinches more skin on her stomach and starts moving it up and down like a horrendous blob of some sort. She smiles, but the look in her eyes betrays her words.

"You're beautiful," I say loud and clear, so she knows I'm not lying. She really is.

"That's really sweet of you to say, Evan."

She looks at her hands. I wonder if she's afraid to look at me.

"I'm serious."

"I know you are." She finally meets my eyes. "I don't know why you like me, though."

"I just do."

"Why did you wait so long?"

"I guess . . . I didn't feel brave until tonight."

"I've seen the way you look at me."

"Really?"

"Yeah, you're not too good at hiding the fact that you're always staring at me."

The Jackets

I reach out and hold her hand. Touching her makes my mind feel foggy, almost like I'm drunk. Her skin's so soft and smooth. I kiss her hand.

"Can I kiss you?" I whisper.

"Yes. . . . "

I lean over and kiss her lips. Slowly at first, then I feel something splash on my hand. I pull myself away. She's crying.

"I'm sorry," Mia says.

"Did I do something wrong? Do I kiss funny? You can tell me, and we can definitely practice until it's perfect," I say anxiously.

"No, no, you kiss by the book. Trust me."

"What's wrong?" I ask as I push a lock of hair away from her forehead.

"It's been a while since I've been touched. It's just a little overwhelming, that's all."

"Oh."

"How long has it been since you've kissed someone?"

"I don't know. A few months . . . something like that. You?"

"A year and a half," she confesses.

"Are you serious?"

"Yeah. Pretty pathetic, huh?"

"But you're always talking to guys. . . . "

"That doesn't mean that they want to date me."

"You flirt with everyone."

"Doesn't mean someone's gonna buy me a drink."

"But you're so pretty."

"Only to you." She smiles as she pulls her sunset-colored jacket closer to her body.

She put me in pajama bottoms printed with monkeys and bananas all over it. Thank God there wasn't a shirt to match.

She stifled a giggle and said, "You look . . . adorable."

Then she broke into a loud laugh, even snorted a little. If she wasn't so adorable, I would've put my jeans back on.

"Are you sure you don't have anything in black? I'll take plaid if you have it," I said.

"Sorry, it was that or my Care Bears pajamas. You can change if you want to."

"No. I'm okay. Monkeys win."

I still couldn't believe I was in Mia's living room. It smelled like flowers . . . at least fake ones in some potpourri bag. I'll never know what it is with women and things that come in tiny little bags.

"Want some hot chocolate?" she offered.

"No, thanks."

We stood there, staring at each other. Nothing else to say. Then she did the cutest thing ever. She bit her lower lip. I couldn't resist. I walked up to her and kissed her. She moaned. I grabbed her butt and lifted her up. She instinctively wrapped her legs around my waist.

"Where's your room?" I asked between kisses.

"Upstairs, first room on the left," she mumbled.

Let me say this. Carrying a woman up a flight of steps isn't as smooth as they make it look in the movies. You need some serious muscle to look like you know what you're actually doing. I have to admit, I broke into a light sweat as I continued to make out with Mia as I climbed the stairs . . . without looking.

I finally made it to her room without stumbling. Now sex was a totally different story.

"You all right?" she asked.

"Fine. Just need a moment."

I smiled, trying my best not to sound like I was having an asthma attack.

"I have to admit. I'm impressed. No one has ever carried me up a flight of stairs before."

The Jackets

"Really? Then I'm going to lie down and look exhausted for the next two minutes." I lay down beside her.

"You're silly."

"I know."

"I hope you're not too tired to kiss me."

"Never."

Brown

"Have a good day, Ma'am." I handed the old woman her bag with a plastic smile on my face.

The old woman didn't respond. She just fluffed her incredibly white hair, pursed her wrinkled lips and walked away without another word. She made me think of an evil version of Barbara Bush. Why do old women wear candy-red lipstick? Don't they know that it runs through the wrinkles above their lips like a red river? Totally gross.

"Drink a little, drive home and wrap yourself around an oak tree," I muttered.

I was working as a cashier in a department store . . . and man . . . did I need to get out of this place.

I looked at Audrey in the booth next to mine. She was giggling.

"You're so bad," she whispered.

She pulled her brown hair into a loose bun and used a yellow No. 2 pencil to help keep it in place.

"I swear, if I get one more person who's rude, I'll quit," I warned.

"Oh, really?"

"Yes, really."

She gave me the tiniest of grins. I stared at the ceiling when I heard her whisper a curse. I glanced over to see her drop all of her Post-it notes and knock down her mug full of pens on her countertop. A total klutz. Always falling and tripping. She always had a visible bruise somewhere on her body. I used to think that it was her boyfriend Keith, but he'd been in to see her before. Cute, blonde and a little too short for my taste, but the sweetest guy.

I flipped through a magazine while I waited for my next customer. It didn't take long for me to get one.

"Hey, Penny. How are you?"

I looked up. It was Joan. She always looked like she had just rolled out of bed and, instead of breakfast, had munched on a live wire.

"Oh, hey, Joan. I'm good. How's it going with you?"

"It's all good," she said as she placed her items on the counter.

I started scanning her things and taking the security tags off some of the shirts she was buying, when she started laughing. I sure as hell hadn't said anything funny.

"That's a mean thing to say," she whispered.

I looked over to Audrey and gave her a confused look and mouthed *What the fuck?*

Audrey shook her head and shrugged.

"Joan?"

"Hang on a second," she said as she pulled a pen and notebook out of her purse and started writing on my counter.

Whatever. I kept my mouth shut and continued scanning her things. I folded her shirts and jeans neatly and placed them in a plastic bag. I punched the total button and waited for Joan to finish.

"No. That's not right," she mumbled as she scratched off a sentence she had just finished writing.

"Forty-nine dollars and fifty cents," I said.

She lifted her face and looked at me. "Huh?"

"Your total is forty-nine-fifty," I repeated.

"Oh, yeah. I have to pay." She nodded and chuckled.

"Who were you talking to?"

"My friend Susie . . . "

"I see."

"You two haven't met yet?" she asked as she handed me her credit card.

"I haven't had the pleasure." I gave her a tight-lipped smile.

"She's really funny," Joan said.

"I'm sure she is." I swiped her card and waited for it to clear.

"There she is." Joan waved excitedly toward the restroom.

I followed her eyes, and there was no one there.

"Where?"

"Over there, by the water fountain," she said.

I wasn't going to argue. I wasn't in the mood. I gave a small wave to Joan's imaginary friend and handed her the slip she needed to sign. She can go and be crazy somewhere else.

"Okay. Well . . . have a good day, Joan. I'll see you around." I handed her the bag of clothes and let out a sigh of relief as I watched her walk out of the store.

"Can you believe that?" I asked Audrey.

"So sad. She's a brilliant writer," she said.

"Really?"

"Yeah. Maybe the crazier you are the better."

"I guess." I went back to my magazine and waited for my next customer.

"Hello," a middle-aged woman said with a smile. She placed all of her things on the counter and waited for me to scan her items.

She wore too much perfume, and her clothes smelled like mothballs. Gross. Her hair was dyed a bright shade of red. There was no way that this woman had locks the color of crimson. I could tell because her roots were salt and pepper. At least she was somewhat polite.

"Did you find everything you were looking for today?" I asked in a polite business-like manner as I continued to scan her things.

The woman's smile vanished. She started complaining about the store and the fact that she couldn't find anyone anywhere to help her. She was using words that no decent human being should use. Wow, I didn't know old people could swear like that.

I was just a lowly cashier. A destitute employee. The bottom of the food chain. The only one that got to hear all of the complaints and any other crap a customer felt like dishing out. I had heard it all.

Slowly I started to walk away from her.

When I realized that the voice was becoming smaller and smaller, I knew that I was as far away as I could manage. I was almost positive that she was calling me a useless bitch and saying things like "How dare she walk away from me?" I knew Audrey would take care of her. I needed to go to my supervisor's office and make *my* complaint. As I made my way to the back of the store, everything became a colorful blur. All I could see was the door.

"Lucy, I'm not doing this anymore," I said as I closed the door behind me and plopped on the chair across from her desk. She arched an eyebrow and locked her brown eyes on me.

"Not doing what anymore?"

"I'm not working here anymore, unless you move me from being a cashier. I'm tired of listening to people complain about stuff they should be complaining about to *you*."

I knew I would probably get fired for this, but that's what I wanted. Because I'm too much of a coward to actually quit. Besides, I could use a few months of unemployment.

The Jackets

"You know I can't transfer you to the floor until I get more cashiers in," she said.

"We have ten cashiers! Ten semi-retarded women that are trained to use a cash register, except Audrey, she's the only one worth keeping around here. How many more do you need? Are you trying to get twenty people that can do in one day what I do in one hour? Come on, Lucy, you know you're just trying to torture me with this stupid job. Transfer me or I'll quit."

This was an argument we've been having for a while. I wanted to be on the floor. Why? Freedom and more places for me to hide from the customers.

"You're bluffing. You know you won't quit."

"Oh, yeah?"

"Yes, now please go back to work before you do something you'll regret," Lucy ordered, rolling her eyes and turning to her computer.

"Fine," I said.

I took a deep breath and, as I exhaled it, I was filled with newly found courage. "I quit." The words echoed in the room for several moments.

"What?" she asked as she looked up.

I repeated myself as I straightened my back and lifted my chin. Defiance, that's what I have to project. Not like I'm big on projecting anything. Usually a hermit, seclusion was always my best asset.

"No two-weeks notice? Just . . . quit?" she stammered.

"Yep." I took off my nametag and tossed it on her desk.

"Okay, nice knowing you, Punky," Lucy said and shook her head.

My nickname really wasn't Punky. Lucy just liked calling me that because it was easier than saying Penelope every five minutes.

"Fuck, fuck, fuck," I mumbled as I walked out of Lucy's office.

"Hey, Pen. Where are you going?" Lawrence asked.

He worked in the electronics department. Cute, but shit for brains. We had dated once, and I almost killed him by the end of the date. He wasn't really a friend of mine, just someone I talked to every once in a while.

"Home," I said.

"Already? It's only eleven-thirty," he said, checking his watch.

"I just quit."

"Holy shit. That's awesome. I'll catch you around then," he said and waved.

Within moments I could sense the whole store whispering. Almost like being trapped inside a beehive. I knew they were talking about me. Of course they were talking about me—what the hell else was there to do around here?

I continued my forced walk, not so sure of myself. The rational part of my brain kept telling me to go back to Lucy and ask for my job back, while the other half gave this place the finger and whistled a happy tune. Over and over, I asked myself, "What to do? What to do?"

I got in my car and rested my head against the steering wheel. I started banging my head against it until I felt a slight throbbing on my forehead. I put the key in the ignition, and my black Honda Civic purred to life. I backed out and drove back to my lonely little house.

My grandmother Melinda had left it to me when I was seventeen. I missed Grandma. She'd saved me from a hopeless life with nothing but anger, hate and a vast emptiness that would've consumed me from the inside out. She'd left me a gateway to a new life.

Of course, my parents weren't happy with the fact that I had a place to run away to whenever they started arguing and

The Jackets

throwing plates at each other during dinner. I guess they needed an audience for their little theatrics. I wasn't impressed. If they hated each other so much, why didn't they get a divorce, like every other normal, miserable married couple? My parents were good people, just not to each other. As soon as I turned eighteen I moved out. It was never my home to start with. Just the place I kept my bed.

I pulled into the driveway of my little white house and marveled at its simplicity. It was a two-story, with dark-blue painted window and door frames. Grandma had a small garden in the backyard, and I took care of it as well as I could. I got creative by adding a few things of my own.

I took my keys out and fumbled for the one that would unlock the front door. Once the door was open, I stepped inside and closed the door behind me. I turned on the lights in the living room and sat down on my poor excuse for a couch. I took off my tired-looking sneakers, peeled the socks off my feet and wriggled my toes. My feet smelled. Good thing I didn't stay all day at work—I would have passed out from my own stench.

I went to the bathroom, rinsed my face with cold water and looked at my reflection while tiny droplets of water dripped off my chin. My eyes always looked so melancholy. It was almost as though I had been crying for days with no end. *Why do I always look so sad?* My friends often asked me if I was okay. When I said that I was, they would give me a strange look and mention that I should smile more often.

How could I possibly smile when my life had become nothing but a series of routines? What was there for me to look forward to? No cool job, no boyfriend, no exciting city, no one, nothing. Why should I smile? Why should I show a fake face to the world? I always had questions. But never any concrete answers.

In the shower, I let out a sigh of relief as the hot water hit my naked chest. I stood under the steady stream and made myself believe that I was washing my troubles away. Forcing them down the drain. I poured some shampoo on the palm of my hand and massaged it into my hair. Some of the soap got in my eyes. I hissed as the suds stung my left eye. I rinsed it off and continued washing myself clean. Water, the only thing that could put me at ease.

I got out of the tub and dried myself with my favorite towel. It was a beautiful moss green. I loved it because it stayed nice and fluffy, no matter what I did to it.

I put on my moon-and-stars pajamas and made myself lunch. Spaghetti and meatballs out of a can, yummy. Sure, it was saturated with sodium and other bad stuff for your body, but that never stopped me from eating it. I was comfortable with the knowledge that I wasn't going to be thin for the rest of my life. I refused to be some anorexic-bulimic-botox-injected-implant-plastic-surgery version of myself.

I poured my saucy, meaty mess into a blue see-through bowl and put it in the microwave. I watched as my lunch bubbled and popped on the spinning plate of this small radioactive oven. The green digital numbers counted down until it flashed END and beeped three times.

"Thank God," I said as I opened the little white door and retrieved my dinner.

"Ooooh, ouch, ouch, hot," I hissed as I played hot potato with the corners of the bowl.

I drew my hand back as I put my food on the table. I shook my hand, hoping that that would shake away the burning sensation from my fingers, and since that didn't work, I shoved my fingers into my mouth. I ate my meal as I checked my email. I had soon wasted two hours visiting miscellaneous Websites and chatting with a few of my friends on AIM. After that I disconnected myself from the Internet and turned off

The Jackets

my laptop. I watched a little TV . . . so many channels and nothing to watch.

I went over my lockdown routine. Locked all the windows and doors. Double-checked everything. Turned off all the lights and went upstairs.

For some reason my book about the Green Man was on the floor next to my bedroom door.

"That's strange," I whispered.

I picked up the emerald book and took a moment to study the cover. His face was painted bright green. He was surrounded by leaves, vines and flowers in bloom. His eyes were the color of golden amber. He had a smile on his lips that led me to believe that he knew something I didn't. I took it with me to bed and read it until I had no choice but to close my eyes.

The earth shook and trembled. It divided itself in two and swallowed me whole. It was a strange feeling, but I wasn't scared. If anything, it was the safest I've ever felt in my life. When I dug myself out, I was covered in dark green maple leaves.

Then all of a sudden a man appeared before me. His skin was made of the bark from the trees that surrounded us. His eyes were a rich earthy brown with gold dust. He smiled, showing his rainbow moonstone teeth. His face was covered in ivy and maple leaves. His hair was a mix of brown and olive vines.

"Hello."

"Hello," I echoed.

He extended his hand to me.

"Where am I?" I asked.

He didn't answer. He stood there and waited for me to take his hand. I reached out and slipped my hand into his and laced our fingers together.

The rest of the dream was a dizzying haze. Almost as though he was hurrying to show me everything in his world before time ran out.

Then everything came to a sudden halt. He leaned forward and kissed me. He pressed his lips to mine. I was surprised at how soft they were, like rose petals. My stomach fluttered as though he had filled it with glowing butterflies. He smelled like ozone, earth and rain.

"Will you stay with me?" he asked.

I hesitated, did not answer, taking a moment to think. "Yes."

I couldn't help but wake up. I turned on my side and gazed at the wall. I wondered what that dream meant. I felt something smooth and hard. I looked down . . . I still had the book about the Green Man in my hands.

The next morning, I remembered my dream. It was so odd and vivid. I spent most of the day thinking about the Green Man's kiss, but I had to set that aside and concentrate on job hunting. Not what I wanted to do . . . but money didn't grow on trees.

I did nothing but drive around, fill out applications and hand out résumé's. No one called. After sitting by the phone . . . the damned thing refused to ring. I guess it didn't help that I did things the way I did. I mean, the right, rational thing for me to have done was to put in my two-weeks' notice and get an extra check in the process. It's a good thing I was only at Whitman's for nine months, so if anyone asked me what I'd been doing I could lie and say "Looking for a job." Which wasn't a total lie. I had looked for employment elsewhere while working at Whitman's.

I liked to think that there could be other possibilities besides getting a job. I could win the lottery, find a box full of money buried by Grandma somewhere in the garden and never worry about work or money ever again. Oh, me . . . and my poor escapist little brain.

The Jackets

The earth swallowed me whole once more. Only this time I didn't dig myself out. I reappeared at the base of a mountain. I walked around until I saw a man surrounded by stags. It dawned on me seconds afterward that he had horns on top of his head that were much larger, more elaborate than the ones on the stags.

He locked his olive eyes with mine. He tilted his head slightly as though not sure what to make of my presence. He approached me. I was amazed with the way he moved. The muscles on his abs moved underneath his skin as though a powerful river raged within him. He was a mature-looking man with long salt-and-pepper locks and the shadow of a beard that matched his hair.

He had a strange necklace around his neck. It was made of knots and intertwined pieces of gold and bronze, and it was open-ended at the front. Each knot was shaped like a different animal.

"It is called a torque," *he said as he pointed to the ornate piece of jewelry.*

"It's beautiful." *I reached out and touched it.*

It glinted in the slight rays of sunlight that filtered through the branches.

"What are you doing here?" *he asked.*

"I don't know."

"What's your name?"

"Penelope."

"I am Cernunnos."

"Where am I?"

"Somewhere between your world and mine. Are you lost?"

"I'm always lost."

"You can stay with me. You'll never be lost again."

"Promise?"

"I promise I'll never leave you," *he said.*

"Then I'll stay."

31

As soon as the words escaped my mouth, my feet sank into the soft soil and turned into dark brown roots. Slowly my body became a laurel tree. All of my branches had gold torques wrapped around them.

I gasped as I opened my eyes. "What the hell was that all about?"

I looked at the Green Man book on my night table. I reached for it. I was going to look through it some more to see if I could find something to explain those strange dreams. But before I could touch it, I started to think. I worried that perhaps it was all because I read the book to begin with.

I pulled my hand away. Now I was afraid of a little green book. None of this made any sense.

I needed to clear my mind. It was a little chilly that day, the promise of fall crackling through the air. It was a jacket kind of day, so I slipped on my brown leather jacket and walked to the park that was a few blocks from my home. It was actually a small forest with a nature trail, picnic tables and a playground. I headed up the damp, cool earth of the nature trail. The tall trees formed jade arches overhead. I breathed the fresh, clean air deeply. I felt instant relief.

Suddenly, I heard the crunching of the leaves just a few steps behind me. My blood froze. I looked over my shoulder and stole a glance at a young man approaching briskly. I slowed my stride and allowed him to catch up in order to get a better look at him.

"Hello," I said.

"Hello."

I looked at him straight on. My heart skipped a beat. His eyes were the color of the dark olives . . . just like the man in my dreams. He had an aquiline nose and thin, shapely lips. He was handsome. He was wearing a black sweater and a pair of loose-fitting jeans. I averted my eyes; I couldn't help but grin at being this close to him.

I continued walking and, inexplicably, bumped into him. I took a few steps back and put my hand on my chest as though doing so would stop it from bursting.

"Oh, my goodness, I'm so sorry," I said.

"It's all right. I wasn't watching where I was going either. I just wanted to ask you your name."

"It's Penelope."

"That's a pretty name."

"Thank you. What's your name?"

"Noah."

"Nice to meet you, Noah." I shook his hand.

It was dry, with calluses on the knuckles. Without realizing what he had done, he laced his fingers with mine, and we started walking together without even thinking about it. I felt as though I already knew Noah. It was as if we were two pieces of the same cloth, finally coming together after being apart for centuries. Somewhere in the back of my mind I was scolding myself for doing something so foolish. But my spirit was completely at ease.

"Do you live around here?" I asked.

"Yes."

"Oh? Anywhere near New London Road? Maybe we can have lunch or something sometime."

"That would be nice."

He told me the things he knew about trees and anything that came from the earth because that's what he loved above all things. He made me want to start humming Nat King Cole's "Nature Boy."

"This is where I leave you, sweet Penelope." He kissed my hand all the while maintaining his eyes locked on mine.

I felt my cheeks redden. His eyes were various shades of green. They made me dizzy with wanting. I shook my head and took a deep breath. I needed to control myself. What the hell was wrong with me?

"What? Well . . . umm, can I see you tomorrow?" I asked.

"I'll find you."

I let go of his hand. My palm glistened with sweat. I did an about-face and took a few steps away from him, but then turned back around to say goodbye.

"Oh!" I shouted when I felt his face right against mine. He pressed his lips over my own. His lips were so soft. I felt every wrinkle, every sweet bit of skin. He kissed me lightly a few more times, caressed my cheek and then walked away. He left me speechless. I wanted to say goodbye, but the words failed me. I wanted to kiss him again, pin him to the ground and take him right there. But all I could do was go home and wait for tomorrow.

The past few days had been absolutely weird. By the time I reached my house, I felt clumsy and awkward.

I went in search of Cernunnos and found a faun instead.

Half man, half goat. He had horns that curled slightly at the end as though they were an afterthought. He was sleeping at the foot of an oak tree. The steady rise and fall of his chest led me to believe that he was resting peacefully.

I snuck up to him and tried to get a closer look. I crouched beside him and studied his face. He had a few black ants crawling over his dark-blonde goatee, but he didn't flinch or try to swat them away. I wanted to pick them out, but I thought it would be rude to wake him from his slumber.

"Would you like a plum?" he asked.

"You're supposed to be asleep," I whispered.

"I can't help it if I can talk with my eyes closed." He smiled.

The Jackets

His teeth were white and yellow, short and perfectly square. He got up and stretched. His fur did very little to hide his manhood.

"You're staring," he said.

"I'm sorry." I looked away.

"I didn't say it bothered me," he chuckled.

"Who are you?"

He smirked at the question as he stood up. He put one hoofed foot forward and bowed gracefully. He stood to his full height and said, "I am everything that is wild, natural and free. I am that untamable urge you have to get undressed in the middle of the forest. I am the whisper in your ear that urges you to do something carefree. I am everywhere and nowhere. I am Pan."

His dark brown eyes glowed as though he had fireflies trapped inside of them. He snapped his fingers and twisted his wrist, producing a plum the color of dark amethyst. It was beautiful. I took it from his calloused hand. I wasted no time biting into it. It was juicy and sweet. The skin was sour, but I enjoyed every single bite.

"Are you lost in the woods? Or are the woods lost in you?" he asked.

"I don't know . . . "

He took his panpipe, which was held by a thin rope slung over his shoulder. He put the instrument to his lips and played a slow, bittersweet melody.

"Why such a sad tune?" I asked.

"Because . . . I'm lonely. . . . "

"I know how you feel."

"Stay with me a while," he said as he offered me his hand.

I looked into his eyes as I took his hand in mine.

Once more, I opened my eyes before I could figure out what the dream meant. There had to be some explanation for all of this.

I ate my breakfast as slowly as possible. I took an extra long shower. I don't know why I was taking so much time to get ready. All I had to do was put my coffee-colored jacket on, tie my shoes and walk out the door. Things are never simple for me when it comes to men.

I got as far as my front yard. I sat down on my bench and gazed at the sky, studied the shapes of clouds. Wondered about the Green Man, Cernunnos and Pan. They were all the same person. But . . . what did he want with me?

I was in the middle of the forest, waiting. I thought about wandering around and going in search of him, but I remembered Noah's words.

I'll find you.

I sat on the soft, moist ground. A cool fall breeze danced by me. I was glad I had decided to wear my dark-brown leather jacket. The moisture went right through my jeans. My panties were damp. Not a pleasant feeling. I stood up and tried to dry myself with a napkin I had in my pocket.

"Hello again," Noah said from behind me.

"Damn it," I mumbled as I tried to cover my behind with my hands.

"Hi," I said.

"What happened?"

"Umm . . . it's kind of embarrassing . . . "

"I doubt that."

I sighed and moved my hands from where they were and showed him my damp butt.

He chuckled.

"Oh, so you do have a sense of humor," I said.

"I do," Noah said.

The Jackets

We stood there for a moment, just looking at each other without anything to say. I looked around and wrung my fingers for a second.

"So . . . shall we?" I finally managed.

He nodded and reached out for my hand. I took it and entwined my fingers with his. I leaned into him, and he wrapped his arm around my shoulders. He was warm. I inhaled the smell of him and tried to hold it inside my lungs for as long as possible. It was a rich spicy musk.

"What did you do this morning?"

"Procrastinate," I said.

"Anything else besides that?"

"Well . . . ," I sighed, "I woke up this morning with nothing to do but come here to see you. And instead of hopping out of bed as though I had a purpose in life, I stayed home and thought. I swear, sometimes I get so frustrated I want to scream."

"So scream," he said.

I looked at him as if he had just asked me to chop my own head off and try to juggle it.

"Go ahead," he encouraged.

I took a deep breath and screamed as loud as possible. I threw my pain up to the sky, trying to reach Heaven with my piercing cry. I wanted to slice clouds in half using just the sound of my voice. For a second I honestly believed I could hear it echo through the trees in the forest. When I closed my lips, I felt lighter, like I could fly away if I wanted to.

That afternoon I told him about my life, my hopes and my fears. And he listened. He would nod every once in a while to show me that he was paying attention, but other than that he never uttered a word. I even forgot I was hungry until my stomach groaned.

Noah smiled. He must have heard it, too. "Would you like to eat at my house?" he asked.

"Where is it?"

"Not too far from here."

I thought about it for a second and then I realized that if he wanted to rape or murder me, he could have done it a while ago, considering how we were alone in the middle of the woods.

"Okay," I said.

I would be lying if I said I wasn't starting to get creeped out by the whole situation. It really wasn't like me to just wander off with someone I had just met . . . especially in an empty forest where no one could hear me scream. I had already tried that, and no one came. It was like the script for a really bad B-movie.

"We're here," Noah said.

We were standing in the middle of an empty field. Okay . . . this was the part where I should have freaked out.

"Umm, Noah? I hate to burst your bubble, but I don't see a house or an apartment or . . . " I tried to control the nervous twitch in my left eyelid.

"Do you trust me?" he asked.

"Not right this second . . . sorry. Nope. You're not really filling me with warm fuzzy thoughts, especially since we're standing in the middle of an *empty* field when you said you were taking me to your house."

"Close your eyes," he whispered.

"No. That's it. I can't do this. I let this go way too far." I put my hands up in the air, turned around and walked away.

"Three times you said yes to me, Penelope. Three times you said you would stay with me. What's so different this time around?"

My blood froze. Oh my God. All of it was real. The dreams. The Green Man. How could this be? It was just a dream.

The Jackets

I thought about what I had back at home. No job. Memories of running away from my parents. My grandmother's kind face. The woman could barely lift a mug, but she could lift my spirits with the tiniest of smiles.

Well, not anymore. I turned around and faced him.

I stood up straight, lifted my chin and tried to keep it from quivering. I closed my eyes. Then I felt Noah's hand on my cheek. He drew himself close to me, and his lips brushed my ear.

He whispered, "I'll never hurt you."

"I'm scared," I said with a trembling voice.

"Don't be."

He was so close, my body grew warm. I felt as though my soul were trying to hum. Noah grabbed hold of my hand and pulled me toward him, my heartbeat racing. I held back the urge to scream.

He held me tightly against his chest and said, "You can open your eyes now. I wouldn't want you to miss this."

I did. I couldn't believe what I saw. Never in my life had I seen so many colors. Everything that I looked at was brighter, more illuminated than anything I could have ever imagined. I slumped down to the ground and tried to catch my breath. My lungs were burning, like I had just finished running a marathon.

"Who are you? What are you?" I asked.

I had my suspicions, but still . . . I wanted to hear him say his name. I needed to know. Otherwise, I didn't think I could ever go back home the same person.

"I'm the Earth Spirit. I protect all things that come from Mother Earth. I have had many names throughout the centuries," he said.

"The Green Man," I whispered.

He smiled and nodded. His head then sprouted green maple leaves.

"Cernunnos," I said.

The leaves vanished with a soft hiss and curved antlers appeared on top of his head.

"Pan!" I looked at him, amazed.

"Yes," he said.

His voice sounded different, distant, almost as if his voice were an echo that had been hidden deep inside his soul for hundreds, maybe thousands of years.

"Where am I?"

The sun was setting in his world, but there were fireflies glowing all around me. There was a white owl sitting calmly on the branch of a great maple tree. And right underneath the tree was a cottage. It had moss in great big patches on the wooden roof and a rough-looking door that was painted bright sapphire. The walls were made of red oak. From a distance it looked like one big piece of brick.

"You came all this way. May as well go inside and take a look."

He walked toward his home and I followed, still in awe. He held the door open for me and, as I walked in, I could feel the peace that was immersed in these walls, a place that had never known violence, anger, hate or defeat. There was a burgundy-colored couch that had a hand-woven blue sheet thrown over it and a table with four chairs. I was surprised by the normalcy of his home. I half expected it to be filled with fairies. It was a beautiful home; anyone would be lucky to live in it.

"Why did you bring me here? Why did you pick *me*?"

"There's something about you. It's in your eyes. They hold a sadness that transcends everything. It pierces my soul. It's something I want to explore for as long as you'll let me," he said.

"Really?"

"You are so beautiful," Noah said as he caressed my cheek.

I found myself leaning into his warm touch.

The Jackets

"Living here, in this cottage, I get lonely." His eyes grew more gray, darker as he spoke. This was his sadness. This was his pain.

"What will happen to me if I stay?" I asked, trying to picture myself as an old woman with long white hair and wrinkly skin next to the eternal youth that stood before me.

"As long as you stay here, you will remain as you are now."

"Forever? You offer *forever* to a woman you met a couple of days ago?"

I parted my lips to say something else, but he stopped me with a kiss. I kissed him back and pulled myself away from him. I ran my fingers through his dark brown hair.

"What do you have to lose?" he asked.

"Nothing . . . and everything. . . . "

I went to the forest one last time. I pulled out the knife that Noah had given me. It was silver with Celtic knots engraved on the hilt. I removed my brown leather jacket and tossed it on the ground. I took a deep breath and held it in my lungs for a moment. I swiped the sharp blade over the palm of my hand and gasped as I watched garnet-colored blood steadily stream from my wound. I let the blood spill all over my jacket. Someone would notice that I was gone, and all they would find was this. I was done with this world. I was leaving my jacket behind, I didn't need it anymore. It wasn't cold where I was going.

The earth shook and trembled. It divided itself in two and swallowed me whole. This is the safest I had ever felt. I was finally free of this world.

Indigo

I stared at him without meaning to. He was perfect. Sand-colored hair, cerulean eyes and tall. His downfall? He looked like the kind of guy that would name each muscle of his six pack . . . he was not smart, but still . . . he was perfect. On the outside anyway. I couldn't help it, my eyes stayed with him. He was that handsome. I don't know why I even bothered. It was like a mouse falling in love with a cat. We were two very different creatures. I wouldn't know what to do with him even if he were remotely interested in me. I pulled out my compact mirror and assessed the damage.

"God," I muttered. "I'm a walking talking bad hair day."

The main reason why I didn't even bother combing my hair every morning was that I knew it would revert back to its usual unruliness within an hour.

"I'm not that bad looking," I said to my reflection, "am I?"

I studied my features in the tiny looking glass in the palm of my hand. Sure my hair could use some work, but if I pulled it away from my face, I might actually be someone worth a double take. My skin was tanned, naturally thankyouvery-much. I didn't do tanning booths. I had chocolate brown eyes. I wish my nose was smaller, but it was distinguished looking. Made me look European . . . I hoped. My lips were full without being over the top. I liked my mouth. I considered it my best asset. Everything else I would trade, except for that.

But there was no chance for me and Mr. So-Called Perfect. The best thing for me was to look away from the handsome American. That's it . . . just look out the window and watch as the cars passed me by. Count all of the black cars, the best source of amusement in this town. Because God forbid that something interesting would happen while I was sitting at The Diner here on Main Street. Welcome to Bumble Fuck, USA. Oh, great, Good-Looking-Guy-Who-Is-Totally-Out-of-My-League is leaving. There was nothing wrong with that. Not like I was going to go up to him and start a conversation any time soon.

"Hey, Joan," Susie said as she walked through the diner doors.

I smiled and waved, which was a lot coming from me. Her curly, red hair bounced happily as she made her way toward me. It was hard for me to show any signs of happiness when I lived in the Middle of Nowhere. I wondered how hard it was for something interesting to happen in my life, other than watching the local beautiful people parade themselves in front of me? I rolled my eyes and sighed.

"Oh, what's the matter now? What existentialist philosophical whatever is bothering you this week?" I looked into the olive-green eyes of my best friend. She really did know me well. One would think that she was made especially for me.

"I don't know." Just on that phrase alone, she'd be able to decipher everything that was bothering me.

"Liar. Staring at the jocks will rot your brain," she said in a sing song tone of voice.

"I am a bad liar, so sue me," I said.

I rested my head on my arm and looked out the window. Anything that was remotely interesting in my life had disappeared last year. After all the shit I'd been through, all I had to show for it was one book. Well . . . one successfully published novel. The others I wrote were published through small presses, and no one even noticed them. All of my other novels combined were nothing like the last one. To be honest, I don't know where I had pulled that story from. All I know is I couldn't have written a word if it hadn't been for Susie.

The end result? I got a lot of money for it. My agent was waiting for me to come up with something else just like it. Only thing was, I hadn't written a word since.

Susie let out an angry sigh and asked for what had to be the millionth time since junior high, "Aren't you hot in that thing?"

I think it bothered her more than anything that I'd been wearing the same indigo jacket since the day we met.

"Leave my jacket out of this. We're dealing with my existentialist philosophical whatever . . . remember?"

"It's like seventy degrees out there. Why don't you enjoy the weather instead of hiding from it?" Susie argued.

"Well . . . it's cool for me." I pulled my jacket tighter against my chest.

"You and that ugly jacket of yours have been running around this town since you moved here. I asked people to describe you a couple of months ago and you know what I got?"

"Do I care?" I asked, tapping my forehead against the table a few times.

I lifted my head only when the waitress brought me a glass of water and handed me a menu.

"Thanks," I said.

I turned to Susie and said, "Proceed."

"That chick with the frizzy hair and the jean jacket." She crossed her eyes and stuck her teeth out.

I couldn't help but laugh.

"Can we order something to eat?" I asked. "Because one of us is actually hungry."

"Not hungry. I ate before I came here."

"Well then, what's the point of us meeting here if you're not gonna eat with me?"

"I'll eat some of your fries."

"Fine."

"I wish you would take that thing off," she muttered.

"I don't care what you say. I only take it off when it's too hot or when I go to sleep."

It was strange how paranoid I had become whenever I took the jacket off. I felt as though something bad would find me. I looked out the window and watched as people passed me by. There was a man that caught my eye, only . . . there was something different about him. He stopped and looked at me. My heart stopped beating for a split second. He had amazing grey eyes. I quickly made myself look away. Susie didn't notice what had just happened since she continued to ramble on about my jacket. I turned my attention back to her and made myself forget about him . . . whoever he was.

"I remember when the sleeves went past your hands and you spent most of the time pulling them up," Susie said, giggling.

Susie loved to remind me of my awkward phases in life. I didn't care what she said. I loved this jacket. It was faded to perfection. It was dark indigo when my mom had bought it for me. I made it my business to wear it every day and get the faded and worn look that was so popular at the time. After a while the whole jacket became a part of my identity. Now, the jacket was worn at the elbows just right. My blue jean jacket was the perfect example of what softness should be. It was the only thing that kept me sane in this retarded town.

"Oh . . . shush you," I hissed.

Susie just laughed louder, which made me smile a little. I liked it when Susie laughed. She had one of those contagious laughs that you knew came from deep inside of her. She could be a pain sometimes, but I couldn't do much of anything without her. She often spent the night at my house while I was writing my novel. She was excellent as a sounding board. I would often run my ideas through her before I made them part of my manuscript.

Some nights . . . I had dreams that a spirit would come into my room and pour words with glowing letters into my mind. I was never sure if it was just the way my mind worked or if someone, somewhere was helping me with my creative process. And if so . . . then who? And why? As soon as I woke up the next day, I would run to my laptop and write.

Susie and I stayed at The Diner and ate and chatted, just like we did every other night. After a few hours, I went home, giving her the same excuse I used every other night: "I have to work on my novel." My nonexistent novel. The novel I had only one chapter of. My agent called every other week and asked how my writing was going along, and I would say, "Fine. Still a couple of kinks I have to work on." Yeah, a couple of kinks being the entire novel that still had no real plot. At least not one that made any sense.

I didn't understand why I had this dry spell. Writer's block, whatever people called it, sucked.

I went home, turned my CD player on and let Mozart fill the silence in my house. I opened the door to my study and waited for the bright light that always washed over me to bleed through the rest of my house. Only there was no light. It looked like a regular room. The shelves held only books, paper and comics. The desk had my laptop and printed copies of my short stories, pens, pencils and a printer. Completely ordinary. I tried really hard not to cry as I sat down by my window, placed my notebook on my lap and waited for an idea to hit me.

This room used to lead to a garden filled with inspiration. Musings, imagination, lyrics, whatever it was I needed. Every creature that used to exist in the old world could be found in this room. When I had finished writing my last novel, this room changed. It was almost as though everything that had made it special dried up. I tried hard to not think so much about what I wanted to write, but why I wanted to write and what kind of story I wanted to tell. Instead of ideas, all that came to my mind were questions.

Did anyone care about things other than sports in this town? Was I at a dead end so early in my life? Was there something wrong with me? Why couldn't I write something worthwhile? Where was God? Why are there so many leaves on the trees? Why couldn't they be ideas that I could pluck away and use? Why did I have to ask so many questions? Thankfully, my thoughts were interrupted when I saw a figure walk by my house. I couldn't really tell what this person looked like, but it was enough to distract me from my questioning mind. It was a man—that much I could tell. He stopped in my front yard. I held my breath and watched as he slowly walked away.

I picked up my pen and notebook. I think I meant for it to be a haiku, but all I wrote was:

I want there to be no more rain in my mind.

"Joan, it's been six months and nothing. What's going on?" my agent Eva was on the phone scolding me as kindly as she could possibly manage.

"I promise you, I'm working on it. Don't worry I'll have something by the end of the year."

I sure as hell hoped that I could write something in the next six months. Otherwise I wouldn't get the hefty advance the publisher was offering on completion of this book because my first one did so well. I wanted to use the money to get the hell out of here. I wanted to leave town. Buy a house somewhere far, far away. Like Paris or Ireland. I didn't care where, just as long as it wasn't anywhere near this stupid fucking town. That wasn't going to happen if I didn't finish this book. Whatever it was about.

"Well, you'd better have at least an outline by the end of the month, Joan. You sent me an awesome first chapter, but I'm still waiting for the rest of it. I can't sell a book with just one chapter," she said.

"Don't worry, I'll have it by the end of the month, Eva," I promised.

"All right, take it easy." She hung up before I had a chance to say goodbye.

She was pissed. Great. Just what I needed, the only woman who took care of my only source of income was mad at me. I wasn't sure things could get any worse.

I was hyperventilating. I could feel my throat constricting. My head was pulsating with pain. I wanted to pull my hair out of my skull in frustration. How could I have been so stupid?

Susie stopped by my house early one morning and asked me to go to the park with her. It was such a nice day, I couldn't resist. I went. I was enjoying the trees, the clouds, the bright blue sky and the sunlight. I loved the way the breeze caressed my cheek and the warmth I felt. But then . . . I started to sweat. It got to the point where I did the unthinkable. Stupid, stupid me left it somewhere. God . . . why? What have I done to deserve this punishment? I should've known better. I felt like a bird without feathers. I had lost my wings.

"Where is it?" I asked.

I could feel the paranoia kick in. Out of the corner of my eye, I thought I saw a shadow run for cover. I thought it would help calm my nerves if I studied the marble statue at the fountain. It was a naked woman holding a crown of laurel leaves in her hands. She had her arms extended toward the sky as though offering it to God as a gift. Then the statue moved.

She slowly turned her face toward me and winked. I gasped. I grabbed on to Susie.

"Oh, God," I mumbled.

"Calm down. I'm sure someone will find your jacket and give it back. No one is going to wear that thing, it's practically molded to fit your body," Susie said.

"Susie . . . the statue moved," I whispered.

"You're being silly. Statues can't move."

"I'm serious. . . . "

Susie glanced at the fountain. The twinkle in her green eyes vanished and was replaced by a darkness I had never seen before.

"Are you all right?" I asked.

"I'm fine. Let's find your jacket and get out of here," she snapped.

"Hey, don't get mad at me. This is all your fault."

"My fault? Excuse me, but you're the weirdo who wears a heavy jean jacket in the middle of summer."

"I took it off somewhere around here, right?" I asked trying to retrace our steps.

"I think so," Susie said, sounding a little kinder than she had a few moments ago.

"I never should've taken it off," I muttered.

"I'm amazed the thought even crossed your mind. Your name is written in the left corner inside the jacket. No one will take it, I promise."

"Are you sure?"

"There is only one Joan Miranda in this town. No one will take it."

She patted me gently on the shoulder. I couldn't help it. I burst into tears. It was more than just a piece of tough fabric for me. It was one of the few constants I had in my life.

"Where could it be?" I asked between sobs.

The Jackets

I began thinking about what life would be like without the damned jacket. Would I turn into a schizophrenic? Muttering to myself all day, answering to voices that weren't there and not showering because someone might be spilling poison into the water? Stupid jacket, where could it be?

"Excuse me, Miss?" someone asked.

I turned around and looked into the grey eyes of someone who seemed familiar.

"Yeah?" I said.

"Is this yours?" he asked as he held my jacket out to me, his hands holding it as though not entirely sure how to.

My hands trembled as I reached out and grabbed my jacket. I smiled and stood there like an idiot, not knowing what to do.

"Say, 'Thank you,'" Susie whispered in my ear.

"Umm . . . thank you."

"Not a problem. I kind of figured it was yours," he said.

Of course, it was mine. I was the only idiot in this town crazy enough to wear a jean jacket in ninety-five degree weather. Plus, the fact that I was crying must've been a dead giveaway.

I liked the sound of his voice. It was deep and comforting. His brown wavy hair reached down his shoulders . . . I wanted to twirl a lock of his hair between my fingers.

I thanked him again as I put my jacket on. I felt comfortable in my own skin now that it was covered. I took a deep breath. I immediately felt more relaxed.

"Before you go, I want to let you know that I almost kept it," he said.

"Really? Why?"

"Because it smells good. A mix between shower clean and day-old perfume."

"No kidding? I don't know what to say. Oh, by the way . . . I'm Joan and this is my best friend Susie."

"Nice to meet you. I'm Malcolm."

We shook hands and smiled for a moment too long. That wasn't so hard. But with introductions over, I wanted to leave. Chit-chat's not my strong suit.

"Well . . . I gotta get going," I said.

"Maybe I'll see you around," Malcolm said.

"Umm, yeah. Sure. I'll see you around."

I waved, and we parted ways. A cute guy gave me my jacket back and told me that I smelled good. Wow.

"That wasn't a total disaster. At least you didn't fall flat on your face and make a total ass out of yourself," Susie said. "Looks like your jacket finally came in handy for once. You should lose it more often."

"Yeah, well the sun must've been shining in his eyes or something. I don't think he would've been that nice had he gotten a good look at me. Unless, of course, he has a thing for girls with untamable hair," I said as I pointed at the top of my head.

"Maybe he does. You never know with some guys."

"Don't try to cheer me up. I just wanna go home. Can we do that?" I whined.

"Yes, Miss Antisocial."

"Thank you."

Susie walked ahead of me, mumbling something. I lagged behind and glanced over my shoulder for a moment. I wanted to see if Malcolm was still by the fountain. I couldn't help but turn around. He was sitting on a bench, staring at the water streaming from the marble statue's mouth. She looked a lot like Susie.

Malcolm must've sensed my gaze. He looked up in my direction and grinned. My heart stopped beating for what seemed like a lifetime. I should've done the same or waved or something, instead of just standing there like a fool.

All I could do was run away.

I found the will to write when I got home. I went to the study, and I deleted that poor excuse of a chapter I had sitting in my laptop. My office still looked normal, but the air in the room felt different. It felt crisp and electric. I wanted that energy all over my body. I took off my clothes and soaked my bare skin in that feeling, that energy. I needed to get it back. I had things to say.

I sat all afternoon and most of the evening writing. I don't know where this new story was going, but at least it was something. By the time my hands were numb, I had forty pages. Six months of being in Writer's Limbo had finally ended.

"So . . . " The phone fell silent and I could tell that Eva had paused to blow cigarette smoke out of her lungs. " . . . what is the story about?"

"It's about a girl who has a hard time letting go," I said.

"Of what?"

I pictured my agent leaning over, putting her elbows on her knees and placing her chin on the palm of her hand. I'd seen her do this every time I said something that she was trying to understand.

"Things like memories, moments, people's faces. . . . She becomes obsessed with writing down everything she sees with great detail because that's the only way she can keep them."

"Why?"

"Because she has a hard time letting go."

"Yes, yes, but you need to tell the reader why. What happened to her that makes her act this way? Otherwise, why should anyone care whether she lets go or not? You need to give the reader a reason to give two shits about this girl."

"Okay," I said, sounding a little glum.

"Hey, you're the writer. I'm just telling you what the editor is going to tell you when he gets his hands on your book."

"Don't worry, Eva. I'll figure it out."

"That's my girl. Call me when you have a hundred pages. Okay?"

"Okay. I'll talk to you soon."

"Bye," then she hung up.

I lay in the middle of a field of sunflowers. It looked endless. Bright yellow petals stared at the sun. I was happy. Everything seemed possible again.

Then a door appeared in front of me. Knock, knock, knock. The sky turned black, and it rained coal.

"No!" I shouted at the clouds.

Lightning cracked and thunder clapped above me.

"No," I whispered as I sat up and opened my eyes.

I was awake. It was all a dream. A very strange dream. Maybe it was a sign. I heard the knock once more.

"I'm coming. Hold your horses," I grumbled.

I opened the front door. Susie was standing on my porch with a paper bag.

"Can Joan come out to play?" she asked with a big smile on her face.

"Do I have to?"

"Oh, my God. You need some sunlight. But . . . before I take you outside, I have to fix that mess on top of your head you call your hair. Come on," she said as she dragged me to the bathroom.

The next hour was one of pure torture. Susie washed my hair, tugged it from one end to the other and applied the old curling iron I had stopped using when I realized how hopeless my hair was.

"Wow," she said as she stepped away.

"That bad, huh?" I asked, dreading to look at myself in the mirror.

"Well . . . see for yourself," Susie said.

The Jackets

I stood up and walked to the medicine cabinet mirror. I gasped when I saw my reflection. My hair was perfectly curled. My locks were now chocolate brown, not the mousey brown hair I was used to. Susie had tamed the monster on my head. I couldn't believe it.

"What did you do?"

"Do you like it?"

"Are you kidding? I love this." I swished my head from side to side and the new curls in my hair actually bounced. I smiled.

"I'm glad you like it, hon. Ready to go outside now?"

"Hell, yeah," I said, feeling much better about myself now that I knew that there was still hope for simple things like my hair.

Always hiding where I can be seen.

I had to remember to write that down somewhere before I forgot it. Sounded like a good way to start a poem.

That's what I was thinking when I saw him again. *Why do I try to hide?* Why did I do this to myself? Someone had to get to know the real me. I couldn't postpone exposing the neurotic mess that I was to the world anymore. God, who was I kidding? The only thing that Malcolm and I had in common was the fact that we had both touched my jacket.

"Well . . . look who's here," Susie said.

"What are you talking about? You told me to meet you here." He frowned.

"Oh, geez, look at the time. Joan, I hate to bail on you like this, but my Mom broke her leg. She needs me and stuff."

"Your mom is dead," I mumbled.

"Doesn't mean it's not a good excuse to leave," she whispered in my ear. "Bye," she sang. Susie smiled and walked away before I could tell her what I really thought about her.

I really hated her sometimes. I turned around and faced Malcolm.

"Interesting," he said as he scratched the back of his neck.

"That's something people say when they have nothing else better to say. . . . " As soon as those words tumbled out of my mouth, I regretted them. Why couldn't I be witty? Why did I have to say the first stupid thing that popped into my head?

"Listen, Malcolm . . . I'm not really good at any of this, so I'm going to spare us both the discomfort of me doing something stupid like putting my foot in my mouth and just go home."

"Can I walk with you?"

"What?"

"Can I walk with you?"

"Why?"

Of all things, I had to ask that? God . . . I wanted to cry.

"Why not?" he asked.

"I'm sorry. I didn't mean to say that."

"Come on, let me walk you home," Malcolm said.

"Okay."

What does one talk about with a stranger? In my case, I could talk about my anal retentiveness and my old desire to shave my hair off. Lucky for me it all made Malcolm laugh. Of course, I am a total klutz, and instead of leaning over to kiss him when he left me at my door, I shook his hand, opened my door as fast as I could and locked myself inside. I took a deep breath and rested my head against the door. What is the matter with me?

He knocked on the door. I assumed that he was still standing out there. I opened the door just a crack.

"Joan?"

"Yeah?"

"Is this going to turn into one of those things?"

The Jackets

"Those you-walk-me-home-and-wait-for-you-and-I-to-kiss-but-don't-because-I'm-not-ready-yet kinda things?"

"Yeah."

"Maybe."

"If you keep putting it off until next time, it's never going to happen," Malcolm said.

"What if I don't want to kiss you?" I asked as I stepped out onto the porch and closed the door behind me.

"You wouldn't have asked that question if you didn't want to." He leaned over and pressed his lips against mine. I had forgotten how soft lips could be. He wasn't in a hurry. He took his time. I pulled myself away from him just to have a second to breathe.

"Do you want to come in?"

"Yeah."

I let him in. He was the first person that wasn't Susie that I allowed past the threshold of my home. I was so tired of being alone. Tired of staring at the same set of white walls every day. I just wanted to be free.

I wasn't searching to be found. Something else I could add to my notebook whenever I got around to writing it down.

Malcolm and I sat on the hunter-green leather couch in my living room. I lit a few candles and let that be our only light.

"What do you want to do with your life?" he asked.

"Travel."

"Really? Where have you been?"

"Nowhere. The furthest I've ever been is New York, and that's only because I see my agent every once in a while to discuss my latest novel."

"Where would you go if you had the chance?"

"China."

The thought of me wearing a straw hat and watching a parade of paper dragons snaking down the street made me smile. All the pictures I would take. All the stories I would write surrounded by all the ancient Asian beauty.

"That's surprising," he said.

"Why?"

"You seem like the type that would say Ireland, or maybe Venice. What do you think is the thing that's really holding you back?"

"You're full of deep questions, aren't you?" I asked.

"You can't answer a question with a question. That's cheating."

I knew the answer to this. I just hated admitting it out loud. "You really want to know?" I fidgeted with my fingers.

"Yes."

I took a deep breath and told him my big secret. "I suppose I'm keeping myself here. I'm comfortable in my own misery, I guess. Comfortable with the predictability of this town and the people who live here. I'm a small-town girl that wants to leave but can't. There's something about this place that's made me stay. I don't know what it is, but it's kept me from leaving for as long as I can remember. Pretty stupid, isn't it?"

"Not really. It's normal to be scared. But it's okay to be brave, too. Maybe you should try that for a change. I think it'll suit you better."

For some reason his words made something in my mind click. Everything seemed possible. I could see myself traveling. Writing everything down in my journal and experiencing the world first-hand, as opposed to learning about everything through the Travel Channel or *National Geographic*.

"So . . . tell me about this novel you're writing," he said.

I laughed and told him to ask me a serious question.

"I am being serious."

"It's a girly book," I warned.

"If it's something you wrote, then I'm interested."

The Jackets

"Okay, if you really want to know. The story is basically about me. Why I need to hang on to everything. I write everything down. Everything I see. Everything I touch. The things I taste. How things feel. And sometimes I write fantasy."

"Why do you do that?"

"I don't know."

It was strange for me to open up to a guy. I liked talking for a change. I wanted to share my world with Malcolm.

"Come with me," I said and stood up.

"Okay."

He followed me to the study door.

"This is where I write," I said.

"Do you sit out here in the hallway or is there something behind the door?"

I smiled and said, "Yeah, just give me a second. The only other person that's ever been in my house besides me is Susie. I'm still getting used to you."

I opened the door. I couldn't believe what I was doing.

"Ummm . . . Joan?"

"Yeah?" I whispered.

"Why is there a centaur in your study?"

"You know . . . normally, there are all sorts of things in here. But a centaur is definitely a first for me."

"You see things like this every day?"

"Not as often as I used to."

The centaur was beautiful. Half man, half horse. He extended his hand out to me. Without words, he was asking me to go with him. If Malcolm hadn't been standing next to me, I would have gladly gone with him anywhere he wanted to take me. Sadly . . . I shook my head. He smiled and, in a flurry of lights, he vanished. My hands ached from wanting to touch the creature.

"What is this place?" Malcolm asked.

"This is where I write."

"This is where your muse lives?"

"I guess. I'm starting to think she abandoned me because this place isn't what it used to be anymore."

"Can you describe to me what it used to be?"

I sighed and took a moment to collect my thoughts. How to describe a place so magical?

"Think about something . . . anything," I said.

"Okay," Malcolm said as he closed his eyes.

"What are you thinking about?"

"The gods at Mount Olympus."

"Okay. Now imagine them doing whatever it is gods do. Imagine their adventures right before your eyes. Think about being a part of that adventure for a moment."

Malcolm opened his eyes and whispered, "Wow."

"Exactly. That's what it was like being inside this room."

"And now it's gone?"

"Yep."

"I'm sorry."

"Me too."

I missed the magic that once had filled this room. More than half of my stories had come from something that was inspired in the study. How could I even think about writing without this place?

"What was your last novel about?"

I couldn't help but smile at the thought of my last novel. It was the one that put my name on the map.

"It's titled *Laurel.* The story of Daphne and Apollo and the things that really happened between them. Why she refused to be with him and how she became a tree. . . . "

"I'll have to pick up a copy."

"Thanks," I replied.

"You know, I think that some of the statues in Greece are the gods," he said.

"Really?"

"Yeah. I mean, who would really carve a giant statue to Diana out of marble and make it look near perfect? Something of that magnitude would take half a lifetime. And who would be able to drag a piece of marble large enough to make a statue? Stuff like that makes me wonder sometimes," Malcolm said.

"That's food for thought."

"Joan, wake up." Malcolm gently shook me awake.

"Huh?" I opened my eyes and realized that I had fallen asleep on his lap.

"Oh, I'm so sorry. I didn't mean to fall asleep. I just wanted to rest my eyes for a moment."

"It's all right. You looked really peaceful in your sleep. I didn't want to wake you up . . . but I have to go."

"Oh, yeah. Of course." I sat up.

We walked to the door and stood there, not knowing what to say to each other. I parted my lips, but instead of words tumbling out clumsily, I got a kiss. I pulled away for a moment and looked into his gray orbs that held dancing lights inside of them. It was like he had fireflies dancing behind his eyes. I kissed him back. For the first time in my life, I felt myself let go of everything that held me down to anything resembling reality.

Malcolm broke the kiss and whispered, "I have to go."

I nodded and kissed him again.

"Goodnight," I said.

"Goodnight."

As soon as he left, I ran to the study and I wrote until my hands ached.

"So, what's the story about?" Eva asked.

She lit a cigarette, pushed her blonde bangs out of her eyes and leaned back in her chair. I actually took the time to drive all the way up to New York to see my agent. There was no need for me to see her in person, what with the Internet, email, smart phones and everything else. But I felt it was important for me to get out of the house for once. She took a long drag from her cigarette, held it in her lungs a few seconds. The smoke swirled out of her nose in little curls.

"It's about a girl named Nydia," I began. "She has a hard time letting go of things. She makes herself go on a sort of quest. Nydia starts writing about everything she sees; she starts to describe the way things feel, taste, smell . . . everything. Until one day she forgets what she looks like, what she likes to do, songs she likes to sing and other things about herself. Nydia forgot herself as she searched for other things."

Eva nodded, which meant that she'd heard everything I said and wanted me to continue.

"She meets a guy named Malcolm," I said trying not to blush, "and he helps her find herself."

"Pretty good. I'm sure there's more to it than just two paragraphs. Is it a novel?" Eva asked.

"Right now it's a novella."

"Well, see if you can turn it into a novel. A novella is a hard sell. But I'll see what I can do."

I handed her the manuscript. At last, I was satisfied with my work.

"What's the title?" Eva asked as she took the manila envelope from my hands.

"Life in the End."

Knock, knock, knock.

I knew it was Susie. It always was her.

"So?" she asked when I opened the door.

"So, what?"

"Where is he? I know he was here," Susie declared as she walked past me and into my house.

"Of course, you knew he would come home with me. You created him. There is no Malcolm . . . just like there is no you."

"Oh no," Susie's eyes widened in surprise.

"There is no you," I repeated, mostly to myself.

"Did you just figure it out?"

Her face started to blur as I tried to erase her from my mind.

"No. I just allowed myself to live a lie. There is no Malcolm. He's someone you created for me, for us." I smiled as I thought about it. A muse's muse. "I guess we both created him. I needed him just as much as you did."

"I'm sorry, I had nothing else to give," Susie said, sounding old and young at once.

"I still love you. I just need to stay away from you for a while . . . maybe forever, I don't know. I want to live a life that is mine."

"He could be real, you know? We could make him so perfect . . . " Susie begged.

Inspiration's final plea. This was why I needed to do this.

"I'm sorry, but you have to go now," I concluded.

I cried as I took off my light indigo jacket and tossed it on the floor. I felt naked, lighter. Twelve years wearing the same piece of clothing. How insignificant it looked, crumpled up on the floor. Why did I wait so long?

"It's okay. I still love you," Susie said sadly.

A crystal clear tear streamed down her blurred cheek. It shimmered as it carved a trail to her chin. I tried to erase her from my mind. Still, she remained, even though I was doing my best to get rid of her.

"What about me? Do I have to go, too?" Malcolm appeared beside me.

I burst into tears as I watched his handsome face begin to blur. If I got rid of Susie, he would go away, too. I think I'll miss him more than Susie. It was Malcolm who had made me realize what I had to do about my life.

"I'm sorry, Malcolm," I said.

"That's okay. You're following your heart. It's what I wanted for you."

"Thank you."

"Don't cry, Beautiful." He reached out and tried to wipe my tears away, but his hand went right through my face as though he were a ghost. He sighed and stepped away from me.

"I guess this is goodbye," he said.

I sobbed and nodded.

"I don't want to go," Susie cried.

She fought and struggled to stay. But nothing she did helped. Slowly . . . they both vanished.

I left my muses behind and picked myself up. I didn't want to wait until it was far too late to become Joan.

Blue

"**D**amn it!" Susie shouted.

She felt the last remnants of her body disappear into the spirit realm. She kept trying to get closer to Joan, but some unknown force kept pushing her away.

"It's no use," Malcolm said.

She slid down to the ground.

"This is your fault. If you had only done what I had told you, we wouldn't be in this mess." She slammed her palms against the floor.

"I didn't want to keep lying to her. . . . "

"Stupid *man*!" She said the word as though it were an insult. "I should've made you a woman instead," she muttered.

"She would've fallen in love with me regardless," Malcolm countered with a smirk.

"Oh? You think this is funny? If we don't find someone to inspire soon, there's a chance you can disappear."

"Me? What about you? You're a muse, too, in case you've forgotten."

Susie looked at Joan. It was as if she was looking at her through a mirror—Joan could no longer see her.

"What do we do now, Susie?" Malcolm asked.

"Don't call me that anymore. That's not my true name."

"What is your real name?"

"My true name is Clio."

Malcolm's eyes grew wide. He could not believe that he was standing beside one of the Nine Muses.

"You're a daughter of Zeus?" he asked in awe.

"One of many."

"What happened to you?"

The muse of history and heroic poetry ignored his question.

"I used to dance on the tips of lightning on stormy nights," she whispered. "I used to laugh whenever the leaves trembled because of the oncoming thunder. I know stories of the mightiest of heroes. Stories that the wind whispers to itself when it wants to remember. Tales that were lost when Troy was destroyed."

"What did you do to Joan?"

He thought of the young writer and wondered how she didn't go insane from so much inspiration.

"I gave her stories no one knew could be written."

"Did she write them all down?"

"Yes. She managed to get some of them published, but the last one that I gave her . . . ," Clio's chest rose up with pride, " . . . was an epic masterpiece. It was genius."

"What's going to happen to her now?"

He stole a glance at the writer. She was starting to become a black outline lost in fog.

"She will write again if she really wants to. Other than that . . . I don't know."

Clio let out a loud sigh. She twisted her red curly hair into a loose bun.

"Let's go find someone that needs inspiration . . . shall we?"

The Jackets

Clio and Malcolm left Newark and wandered from town to town looking for writers that showed promise. When they reached New York City, Clio thought she had found a man with immense potential, but he let his girlfriend get in the way of his passion.

"You see? That's why Joan was perfect," Clio commented to Malcolm as she walked away from the writer.

"How so?"

"There was no one to stand in her way. No one to tell her to stop daydreaming. No one to boss her around. No man to interfere with her dreams."

Malcolm was not sure why he had decided to stay with Clio. She was definitely not pleasant. She spent most of her time looking for another author like Joan or talking about how perfect she was. He thought about the little time he had managed to spend with Joan. She had seemed trapped in a dream world, and he had felt sad for her. Clio had had such a firm grip on her.

He smiled as he remembered their first kiss. He often wondered if it was real or if it was something that lived only inside of Joan's mind. Now, he was a muse who had no one to inspire. He was a man in love with a woman with whom he could never share a life. Now, he was stuck with an immortal muse, and they were both futilely in love with the same woman.

"You loved her, didn't you? More than a muse should. That's why you're so angry."

Clio stopped as though someone had nailed her to that particular spot. The only movement in her body came from her shaking fists.

"You love her still."

"Silence," she hissed, turning her head.

The only thing Malcolm could see was her striking profile.

"That's why you stayed with her for as long as you did," he said.

"I said silence," she said louder.

The clouds above them turned grey. The smell of ozone invaded his nostrils. The rumble of thunder soon followed.

"You stayed with her so long that you couldn't inspire her anymore. You stayed with her until you nearly drove her mad with loneliness," Malcolm said.

"Silence!"

Clio grabbed him by the neck and lifted him up in the air. She squeezed his throat until he turned bright purple. Lightning flashed in front of his eyes several times.

Clio drew his face close to hers. "You will not speak of this any further," she commanded.

Malcolm managed to nod. Clio released her grip, and he fell to the floor.

That night, Malcolm left Clio while she slept. He didn't know where he was going or what he would do when he got there, but he knew that he could not stay with her any longer.

"Malcolm?" Clio called out when she opened her eyes the following morning.

"Malcolm? Where are you?"

She looked for him for days and could not find a trace of him anywhere.

I'm all alone.

Malcolm went back to Newark and looked for Joan. He went to her house and found that it was empty. Joan had boarded up the house and left town. She was gone.

He went back to the park where they had met for the first time, the place where he touched her faded indigo jacket. It was a sweet moment. He didn't know why he had been so happy that day.

"It's because you were physically holding something of hers," a voice said.

"Who said that?" Malcolm asked.

"I did."

The Jackets

A bolt of lightning cracked a foot away from where he stood. When the smoke cleared, before him stood the tallest being he had ever seen.

"Who are you?" he asked.

The man in front of him had long white hair that fell to his shoulders in curls and grey eyes that looked like clouds before a storm. The immortal smiled, and Malcolm saw lightning dancing inside his eyes.

"Zeus," Malcolm whispered.

"Yes," he said.

"What are you doing here?"

"Assessing the damage," Zeus said as he studied Malcolm.

"What do you mean?"

"Where is my daughter?"

"Clio?"

Zeus nodded.

"I left her in New York after she tried to kill me."

Zeus chuckled as though Clio killing him was nothing more than a child having a tantrum. "Ah, yes. She's always had a bit of a . . . temper. Interesting . . . "

"What is?" Malcolm asked.

"You are."

"How so?"

"Clio created you, correct?"

Malcolm nodded.

"It is interesting that my daughter, who has numerous times told me how much she abhors me, would create a man in *my* image."

Malcolm thought about what Zeus had said and realized that his own eyes were the same color as Zeus's. And his hair, although it was brown, was the same texture and length.

"Why do you think she did that?" Malcolm asked.

"I don't know. I suppose I will have to go find her and ask her myself. But before I do that, who were you looking for?"

"Joan," he barely mumbled.

"The woman she stayed with for so long?" Zeus frowned.

"Yes, I don't know how to find her."

"Hmmph. Let's say you find her. Then what? She can't see you anymore. Especially if she willingly made you disappear. Will you follow her for the rest of your life? You will disintegrate into thin air from not providing inspiration to those who need it."

"But . . . I love her," Malcolm said.

"Very well . . . "

There was a flash of light and then everything went black.

Dear Journal:

I have finally arrived! I am in Barcelona, Spain. I decided to come here to finish the second half of the new novel I'm working on. I sent the novel I just finished, Life in the End, *to Eva, and now she's trying to get a new deal with my publisher. Although my mind and my hands are busy, for the first time in my life I feel as though my heart is at peace. I guess Susie was a lot of weight to carry on my shoulders. I do miss Malcolm though. There's no other way for me to explain, I just miss him.*

Joan looked up from her journal to take in the view of the Mediterranean before pouring more of her thoughts into her journal. She thought she saw a familiar face among the crowd on the beach but shook her head and returned to her pen and paper.

For a moment I thought I saw him. But that can't be. Great . . . now I can add "hallucinates" to my list of flaws.

She looked into the crowd on the sandy shore once more. Joan squinted, trying to will her sight to get a closer look. She stood up and walked toward the man.

"It can't be . . . " she whispered.

When she saw him smile, she knew it was him.

"Malcolm?"

"Joan!" he shouted as he broke into a run.

"Oh, my God." She smiled and ran toward him.

They both stopped an arm's length from each other.

"Hi," Malcolm said.

"Hi."

"I've been looking for you . . . "

Joan pressed herself against Malcolm and kissed him. Her heart fluttered as she felt his warm lips upon her own. She parted her lips and slipped her tongue inside his mouth. He held her tighter against his body. He inhaled and took in the smell of her. He couldn't believe that he was with her at last. He pulled away from her and caressed her face.

"How?"

She ran her fingers through his brown hair, still mesmerized by the sight of him.

He smiled and replied, "Let's just say I have a new friend who can do almost anything."

"Is this real? Are you real? Or is this all in my head again?" Joan touched his face and tried to confirm his existence.

"Why don't you ask that man if he can see me?" he suggested as he pointed to an elderly gentleman sitting a few feet away from them with a sketch book on his lap.

Joan frowned at the suggestion, but approached the man and asked, "¿*Usted puede ver el hombre parado ahí?*"

She pointed to Malcolm. The artist looked where she was pointing and nodded. Joan grinned and thanked the old artist. She turned around and went back to Malcolm.

The old man stood up and smiled. When he was sure they weren't looking, he disappeared inside a bolt of lightning.

"What does this mean?" she asked Malcolm.

"I don't know. It may be the smartest thing or the dumbest thing I've ever done. Either way it doesn't matter."

"What happened to Susie?"

"You don't have to worry about her anymore."

Joan let out a sigh of relief. She leaned in for another kiss and listened to the ocean hiss against the sandy shore. She was finally happy.

Zeus smiled. He was walking down the streets of New York City wearing a white shirt, stylish jeans and black boots. Though his hair was gray, his looks had never faded. He was slim, fit and tan. He had the appearance of a man that spent most of his time sailing across the sea. He could feel the stares from passersby, both women and men. When he had more time, he would be more than willing to have a quick romance with a few of the women that caught his eye. But at that moment he was looking for his estranged daughter. He could sense her close by.

Zeus stopped in front of an art gallery.

Here you are, he thought as he entered the building. There was a tiny stage all the way in the back of the gallery. He glanced at some of the artwork on the walls. Most of it was solid colors with a black vertical line across the canvas. He shrugged his shoulders and quickly lost interest.

In front of the microphone was a tall, voluptuous woman. He stayed as far away from the crowd as he physically could. He pressed himself against a wall and listened to the woman recite her poem.

*My father murdered
my little brother
when he was a child.*

*Not in the physical sense.
It was an emotional killing
he performed.
There were no
scars, no proof to show*

The Jackets

the world what had
been done to him.

He stripped this little boy
naked and forced him
to grow up.

Sometimes I wish
I could've done more for him.

My father . . .
our father, the pirate.
I hope he's proud of
what he's done.
I hope he knows that
not all little boys grow
up to become pirates.
Not all little boys
who start out as
Lost Boys
grow up and
become Lost Men.

When she finished, everyone applauded. Zeus surprised himself by clapping along with everyone else.

"She's talented, don't you think?" Clio asked as she appeared beside him.

"Not bad for an amateur, I suppose. Poetry was never something that interested me. Did you help her with that?"

"Just a little. She did the rest herself. When there is pain, people tend to want to express themselves even more than when they are content."

Zeus looked at his daughter and smiled. He was happy to see her.

"What are you doing here?"

"I was worried about you."

"You? Worried?" she scoffed.

"I am your father. Whether you like it or not."

"What are you really after?"

"I would like for you to come back home. I believe it's been long enough. You've proven your point."

"I don't want to go back."

"Suit yourself," he conceded.

He shook his head. He didn't want to push her into doing something she didn't want to do. He had hoped that she would reconsider. He opened the gallery door just as another poet took the stage. He stopped himself for a moment and said, "I saw your friend Malcolm recently. He reminds me of someone I used to know."

"That traitor? What did he have to say?" she snapped.

"He had the most interesting request," he said with a grin.

Zeus knew exactly what he was doing. The woman was Clio's Achilles' heel

"Really?"

"Yes, something about a girl, Joanna or something. I can never really keep up with names these days." He sighed and vanished before Clio could muster up the courage to ask him anything else.

"Joan?" she whispered.

When Clio peered through a window of Joan's new home and saw Malcolm, her heart shattered into a thousand pieces. As they danced, the warm orange glow of sunset shone upon Joan's skin and hair. She looked beautiful, like someone had sprinkled bronze powder over her entire being. Her locks neatly tied into a bun, they were finally under her control. Joan rested her head on Malcolm's shoulder, and he kissed her lovingly on the top of her head.

The Jackets

This can't be.

She ran. She sped away from Joan's house as fast as she could, infuriated. She finally stopped to catch her breath, her lungs on fire.

"Father!" Clio shouted at the sky. Within moments, a flash of light transported her to Mount Olympus.

The throne room was filled with gods and goddesses. It was strange to be among her own kind once more. She watched beautiful Aphrodite blowing kisses at the vengeful savage, Ares. Penelope was in a corner, still crying over Odysseus and his constant infidelities. Pan was dancing from one end of the room to the other while playing his panpipe. Clio noticed that there was a mortal woman following Pan. There were too many gods to name, all of them amazing in their own way.

Her father was seated on his massive black marble and leather throne. He had several women and nymphs gathered around him. One of them was feeding him green grapes.

"Yes?" he asked without giving his daughter a glance.

"How could you? You gave something to Malcolm that you could have given me. Why did you give him mortality?"

Zeus sighed and shooed the women away. They huffed and moaned as they ran off.

"Why would I do that to *my* child? Malcolm was but a wisp of a thought. Close to nothing. He'll be dead in the time it takes me to blink. Why would you want that?"

"You gave him everything I ever wanted," Clio replied. "I will never die, that is true. But you have cursed me to an eternity without love. I have had to stand by and watch lovers and friends wither and die. All I ever wanted was to die alongside them. I'm tired of being this world's historian, a keeper of stories no one wants to hear."

"Love? I know plenty of it. All it does is fog up the mind and complicate everything," Zeus countered. "Look at what love has done to you. You could have been great. You could have inspired the whole world to be more than what it has become. Instead you come crawling to me rambling about love. For a woman, no less.

"Look for Hercules, and see if you can make something out of him. Make yourself useful and help an archeologist dig up an ancient scroll. Teach this world a thing or two about how we did things before they invented their precious technology. But do not plague me with anymore requests to become mortal."

"Father . . . please," she pleaded.

"I said NO!"

A gust of wind blew into the throne room and carried Clio outside the gates of Mount Olympus. She laid down on the rocky ground and wept. Tiny silver stones dug into the palms of her hands. Crystal clear tears fell and became lost in the gravel and filtered through to fall to Earth as rain.

School had let out for the day, and Clara sat on the bench waiting for her mother to pull up. The cool wind of autumn made her happy she had her mom's old azure jacket on. All of her friends wanted to borrow it, but she wouldn't let anyone come near it. Clara loved the jacket because it smelled like her mother, even after she washed it.

"Hi. Mind if I sit next to you?"

Clara turned her blue eyes toward the voice. It came from a short, red-headed girl who looked to be about fifteen years old, the same age as Clara.

"Go ahead. It's a free country."

"Thanks," the girl said as she took a seat.

Clara let out a loud sigh just as her cell phone rang. "Hello?" she answered the tiny silver flip phone.

The Jackets

After a thirty-second conversation, she said, "Okay, love you too," and pressed the off key.

"Is she late?" the girl asked.

"Yep," she said dryly.

Clara wasn't in the mood for small talk. She was hoping that one-word responses to the girl's questions would shut her up.

"Nice jacket," she commented.

"Thanks."

The girl took a closer look at the blue jean jacket. She could've sworn that she had seen it somewhere before.

They sat next to each other in an uncomfortable silence. Clio smiled as she looked at Clara, knowing there was something special about her. She could feel it in her energy. She closed her eyes and soaked some of it in. She wished Clara hadn't been so rude, making it harder for Clio to see whether she had any true talent or not. For a moment Clio thought she saw a name scribbled on the inside of Clara's jacket. Her heart stopped.

Clara leaned forward. She thought she caught a glimpse of her mom's dark green Mustang. Clara stood up just as her mother's car pulled up. She gracefully opened the passenger door and slid onto the smooth leather seat.

Clio ran in front of the car and said, "Joan? Joan Miranda?"

Clara's mother rolled the window down and stuck her head out. "Yes? Can I help you?"

She didn't recognize the young girl standing in front of her car.

"She's weird, Mom," Clara mumbled.

"I can't believe it's you. After all these years." Clio slowly walked toward Joan. *How long has it been? I was only at Olympus for a day.*

"I'm sorry. Have we met?" Joan asked.

"I'm Clio." It was only after she said her true name that she realized that it wouldn't mean anything to Joan, since she had known her as *Susie*.

"Mom, can we go?" Clara insisted.

Has it been that long? Clio slowly walked to the driver's side and looked at Joan for the first time in fifteen years. She smiled as she noticed the crow's feet at the corners of her eyes and the grey strands in her hair.

"Yeah, let's go," Joan said to her impatient daughter.

"Goodbye," Clio whispered as she stepped out of the way.

"Bye, bye," Joan said with a small wave as she drove away from the school.

Joan felt a chill run through her as she drove away from the girl. There was something about her. . . . she just couldn't put her finger on it.

Clio returned to Joan's house. There she saw Malcolm. He looked older, but still handsome. His hair was salt and pepper and he wore wire-rimmed glasses. She stood on the tips of her toes and looked into their house.

Malcolm whispered something in her ear, and Joan filled the house with her laughter. Clio couldn't help but smile. Joan had such a wonderful laugh, so infectious.

Clio burst into tears. Her heart was finally broken.

Joan yawned and stretched as she stumbled to the window the following morning. She drew the curtain open and looked at her front yard. She frowned.

That's strange. What's that?

She put a robe on and headed downstairs, went outside and looked at the marble statue that had appeared there overnight.

"Oh, my God," Joan gasped. "Malcolm!"

The Jackets

She ran inside the house and called out to him again. She heard him stumble out of bed. He rushed down the stairs and almost tripped on the last step.

"What? What is it?" he asked as he put his glasses on.

"Look." She pointed to the lawn.

Malcolm squinted. He couldn't believe his eyes.

"I guess she finally found you," he whispered.

He took a deep breath and went outside.

"Honey?" Joan asked as she followed him.

"Yeah?"

"Is it Susie?"

"Yes."

He took a step back and studied the marble statue that now decorated their front lawn.

"How did this happen?"

"Grief," he replied.

Malcolm noticed something shimmering at the statue's feet. He got closer and saw that there were tear-shaped diamonds all around her.

"What are those?"

"Diamonds, or tears. Both. I don't know." He picked one up and inspected it. It was a blue diamond . . . with water inside of it.

"She stood here and cried all night?" Joan asked in disbelief.

"I guess."

"Why didn't any of us see her? Why didn't I hear her?"

"Remember, you forced her out of your life. Once that happens, she can't come back."

"Well, we can't just leave her here."

"What do you suggest?"

"I'll make a garden in the backyard. We'll put her there until she wakes up," Joan replied.

"If that's what you want to do . . . "

"Do you think she'll ever wake up?"

"It all depends on you. You have to really mean it, though," he explained.

"I see."

"Do you think you can handle that?"

"I think so," Joan answered not too confidently.

Over the next few months, Joan worked every day on her backyard to create a garden for Clio. The white marble statue of the beautiful muse stood in the center of it all. She put in a koi fish pond and planted rosebushes, lilacs, lilies and tulips that would all bloom in late Spring.

"I hope you wake up soon," Joan whispered into Clio's marble ear. "I'll be waiting for you, old friend."

Grey

Death wrapped its cool arms around the shell I called my body and led me to the warm light of Heaven. I felt the warmth envelop my soul. *How had I lived so long without this feeling? This warmth?*

Something or someone was beating my chest, forcing a heartbeat out of me, followed by another and another. . . . each painful beat reminded me of my mortality and how close I had come to being in Paradise.

I opened my eyes. The glare forced my eyelids to close again. I struggled to open them once more. I was in a hospital. I could smell my mother's perfume—she had to be close by.

"She's awake!" my mother shrieked.

I knew it. Damn! I tried to speak but that was taken away from me, too. I couldn't even tell my mother to leave me alone.

"Don't speak. This whole week has been a nightmare. You were dead for a couple of minutes," Mom instructed me.

I wish I'd stayed that way.

I didn't even know what had happened. Death's cold fingers had brushed over me for a moment, only to leave me longing for them once more. My dad brought me a glass of water and put a straw to my lips. God bless him. He always knew when to stay quiet. I only wished Mom would follow his lead every once in a while. I drank several sips of water. My dry throat thanked me with every drop I swallowed.

I cleared my throat and said, "Mom, shut up."

"Emma!" Mom squawked.

"Come on, sweetheart, let's leave her alone," Dad said as he put his hands lovingly over Mom's shoulders and led her out of the room.

"We'll see you in the morning, kiddo," he said as he walked out the door. Dad understood what I was going through.

I got hit by a car. At least that's what the chatty nurse said when I asked how I had gotten to the hospital. Well, a car is too general a phrase . . . it was more specifically an SUV. Not a regular one either. One of those ugly squared ones that looked like a five-year-old drew it at school during recess. I died because of a giant toy car. No wonder I was brought back to life. After Death had a good laugh, he decided that I didn't deserve to die that way.

This is how messed up I was:

Both my legs were broken.

One rib fractured.

A concussion, which is probably what killed me.

I kept trying to remember that day, but all I could go back to was that heavenly light.

Andrew showed up the following week. I felt like I should pretend to have selective amnesia. There was something about the way he looked at me. He had guilt written all over his face. Why couldn't I remember that day? Why was he looking at me that way?

"Emma, good, you're okay," he said with a sigh of relief.

"Yes, I'm okay. Why wouldn't I be?" I said with a bright sunny smile. This was going to be fun.

"Listen, I came here . . . " he started to say.

The Jackets

"I'm sorry. This is awkward," I interrupted.

"What is?"

"Do I know you?"

"What?"

"Do I know you?" I repeated.

"Are you serious? We lived together for three years."

I know.

"We worked in the same building for a year."

I know.

"I was there when you got hit by that car," he finally said.

Now, that I didn't know. Interesting. No one here had told me that bit of information. It brought on a whole new set of questions. What was he hiding? If Andrew loved me so much, why wasn't he here when I woke up a little more than a week ago? Even more interesting.

"What's your name?" I wanted to know if he'd give me his real name. This was fun. I suppressed the urge to giggle.

"Andrew."

"We'll, that's half of you, Andrew. No last name?"

Was he trying to take advantage of me? *Come on, keep sweating, you bastard. Lie, I dare you.*

"McNeil, my last name's McNeil."

Good answer.

"Well, now that we've cleared that mess up. Andrew, I'm breaking up with you. I want the keys to our apartment, which I'm still paying rent for. I'm going to call my father to make sure all your crap is out by the time I leave the hospital," I announced.

"Are you playing with me? Because if you are, it's not funny."

"No, I'm not playing with you. If you need proof that I don't have amnesia, here it is. Your birthday is April 23, 1979. You have a birthmark on your inner thigh in the shape of a strawberry. You hate *Wayne's World*, which doesn't make sense because that movie's awesome. You hate my cooking and you like to drink milk one day before the expiration date."

"That was cruel."

"I know," I said as I pointed to the door.

"Okay, I guess that's that."

He lowered his head, his dark brown hair covering part of his face like a curtain. He was handsome, I granted him that. But having him in my room just didn't feel right. He was a piece of a puzzle that didn't fit in with the rest.

"You left this in my car." He tossed a neatly folded grey cloth onto the bed by my hand.

We looked at each other for a moment, and I was surprised to see that he was genuinely sad over the whole thing. I regretted my decision for a flicker of a moment, but turned cold once more. I knew I'd be changed because of this accident.

I looked at the folded metal-grey jacket that he'd left by my side. He shoved his hands into his jean pockets and walked out of the room.

My jacket. The last time I wore it was the day of the accident. I pulled the jacket tight to my chest as I remembered the day I had died.

The day of the accident was a gorgeous fall afternoon. A little too crisp for my taste, which was why I wore my jacket. Andrew and I had been having problems over the past few months. Which was basically him cheating on me—on *my* bed, on *my* sheets, in *my* apartment.

Andrew had picked me up at a quarter to noon to have a nice lunch and try to work things out. I was enjoying hating him at that moment, which was why I was being difficult on purpose. I wanted to make him suffer, so I tried to make the feeling last for as long as I could. He had the heater turned on a little too high, and I took my jacket off and rolled down the window to get some fresh air in the car. We argued on the way to the restaurant.

"Why don't you go fuck yourself?!" Those were my last words to him, at least they would've been if I'd have stayed dead.

At a traffic light, I jumped out of the car and crossed the street without looking both ways. Andrew shouted a warning. I turned around just in time to see a silver car coming at me.

Pain.

Release.

Peace.

Only to have pain once more.

Did I regret letting Andrew go the way I did? No. There were more where he came from. I was pretty sure he'd find someone else who'd make him feel special for ten minutes. It just wouldn't be me . . . ever again.

Black

The sky was slate grey. Fall would finally make way for winter's bitter wind. I should've worn something other than my black leather jacket, at least a sweater or something. I had no car, but I had the best pair of legs in town because of it.

I climbed up three flights of stairs while carrying a few bags filled with groceries. By the time I reached Emma's apartment, I was panting. I kicked the door lightly. I had a key, but I just believed that Emma could walk a few extra steps during the day, if only to open the door for her best friend.

Emma had been in a really bad car accident, breaking her legs and injuring other body parts in the process. I just wished she would try to get around a little more. She could walk with the help of a cane, but she preferred to sit in a wheelchair for most of the day and stare out the window. She didn't go out unless it was to the doctor's office, and that didn't happen too often either. She always had an excuse for not going to the doctor or physical therapy. I wish I knew what had happened to her the day of the accident. What made her give up on life?

I set down some of the bags and waited. No movement. Not a peep came from inside the apartment.

"Emma!" I shouted as I pounded my fist on the door.

I knocked and rang the doorbell several times. Why was it so hard for her to open the door? I gave up and pulled the keys out of my purse and unlocked the door. I picked up the groceries, went in and put the items I purchased for Emma in their proper places. Then I opened the windows to let some fresh air into the apartment. I hated that stale smell her place got when the windows have been closed for too long. I walked around the living room, straightening things out. I was picking up a few magazines by the futon when I noticed Emma's smooth bare legs sticking out from underneath a grey blanket. I pulled the blanket off her head and smiled to see her normally straight black hair in disarray.

Emma had been a pain in the ass about her hair, getting a haircut every month. Her nails were always manicured. She always smelled so nice. Like lavender. Now she smelled of day-old clothing and sweat. I'd never seen her like this. But even though she wasn't exactly at her best right now, my heart still skipped a beat every time I was near her. All I ever wanted to do was love and take care of her. I shook my head—she wouldn't reciprocate those feelings. She had said so in the past. Not because of anything I said or did. It was just one of those comments she made while we were hanging out. So, for now, I would continue to love her as a friend.

I took off my leather jacket, set it on top of the stool in the kitchen and went about my usual business. I went to the bathroom and pulled out the toilet brush, the sponge and cleanser. I cleaned the tub, the shower walls and the toilet. It was a sucky job, but it was the only way I knew how to help her.

I hummed Queen's *Somebody to Love* while I straightened things out in her room and made her bed. I stopped working and noticed that her place was strangely quiet. Something was wrong. Emma wasn't awake. She always woke up from whatever coma-inspired nap she was having to at least say something to me. Even if it was a smart-ass comment or mumble about how much she wanted to die already. That's what scared me the most, the things she would say underneath her breath.

I slowly walked down the hallway until I reached the living room where she slept. She was laying face up, her lips slightly parted as though she had a secret she wanted to whisper in her sleep. Her lips were deathly pale.

"Oh, God. Please be alive. Emma. Emmie, please be alive. Please, please, God," I whispered as I got closer and checked her pulse.

Someone should've checked mine. It was going at a million miles per second.

Just as my hands touched Emma's wrist, her eyes opened wide, almost showing the white in her hazel eyes. I leapt back five feet and screamed.

"I'm not dead, you idiot. I can't go to Heaven if I commit suicide. At least that's what the priests say. . . . Just another way of running away," she grumbled as she sat up.

"You crazy . . . bitch. You scared the living shit out of me," I said as I put my hand over my heart.

I was lucky I didn't have a panic attack. That would've made this day . . . much more fun.

"You should've known better than to think I'd do something like that," Emma said.

I walked away. I went to the kitchen and poured myself a glass of water. I drank it in three gulps. It's always hard for me to be so close to her. It's almost like I have to struggle even more not to touch her. To not say what I really want to say. I guess you never get over being in love with your best friend.

"What's wrong, Faith?" she asked.

"Nothing a shot of whiskey can't fix."

"Listen, I'm sorry about that. I was being an ass. It wasn't funny," she confessed.

"Emma?"

"Yes?"

"Can I ask you something?"

"Yeah . . . "

"What was it like?"

"What? Dying?"

"Yeah, what was that like?"

She pressed her lips together. It made me wonder if she wanted to keep those words inside her mouth a little longer before releasing them into the room.

"Have you ever stared at the sun for far too long and then you look away? You get sun spots in your eyes?"

"Yeah . . . "

"I feel like I'm living life with sunspots in my eyes, day in day out. I can't do anything except wish to stare at that light once more. Do you know what it's like to know that you have a place in Heaven and to be denied entrance? I understand that it's not my time, but it doesn't make living any easier. This life is hell, Faith. This life . . . it's hell. And all I want to do is stare at the sun all day long."

She laid back down and pretended to be dead by looking at the ceiling. I didn't know what to say. I felt like I had nothing to give my friend that would make her feel better or lighten her load.

"I don't believe that, Emma," I said finally.

"You don't understand."

"And that's okay. I probably never will. But you can't sit there and tell me that life isn't worth living. What's so great about sitting in your apartment, and waiting to die? Do you know when that's going to happen? Most likely when you're one hundred years old and half of your teeth are missing. How long is your list of regrets going to be then? Would you rather hide or live the best way possible? I don't know about you, but hiding sounds cowardly to me. I never knew you to be a coward, Emma."

The Jackets

"I *am* a coward. Most of my life was just an act. I pretended to be things that I am not. That's why *my* life is a lie, nothing but make-believe. God, I don't want to do this anymore. Faith, I'm so tired."

"Don't talk like that. Come on, let's go outside. Why don't you come to the park with me? It's a little chilly, but it's nothing you can't handle if you put on a sweater or something."

She sighed and said, "I'd rather not. At least not today."

"Fine, do you need anything else before I go? Foot massage? Sponge bath?" I waited for her to say "No" like she always did.

"No, thank you."

Like clockwork, she never missed a beat.

"Then I guess my job here is done." I grabbed my purse and headed for the door.

"Why do you do that?"

"Do what?"

"Ask me if I need anything, stay for a few seconds to make sure I'm all right and then leave. Why do you run off in such a rush? I know you don't have anything else to do. Am I that awful that you don't want to spend any more time with me?"

"I don't think you can handle the answer to that question," I said.

"Try me . . . "

"Fine."

"Fine," she echoed.

"I love you."

I said it. I couldn't believe it. The words had been burning in the back of my throat for three years. I had had to avoid saying anything to her since I first realized my feelings for her.

"I know you do. Now, how about you answer my question?" She had missed the full meaning of what I had just said. She thought I meant friendly love.

"*You* don't understand," I tried to explain.

"What don't I understand?"

The confusion on her face made her seem so much more beautiful to me. Tears welled up in my eyes. Why couldn't she be a man? That way I could just kiss her and know that it would be all right. No questions asked.

"I'm in love with you," I whispered.

Emma studied my face for a moment, all the while processing what I had just said. Her hazel eyes met my brown eyes. Her face changed one moment at a time as confusion changed to knowing. Now she understood.

"How long have you felt like this?" she asked.

"Three years."

"Wow."

"I remember the exact day, too."

"Really? Can you tell me?" she asked as she sat up and gave me her full attention.

I smiled as I conjured up the memory. "It was that night you had an argument with Andrew. You were thinking about breaking up with him. You came over to my house, and a whole bunch of our friends were there. But you only wanted to talk to me. We walked around the neighborhood for a while. Then it started to rain. It was pouring that night.

"We could barely see what was in front of us. But you didn't care . . . so we kept walking. By the time we came back to my building, we were soaking wet. I noticed your shirt sticking to your chest. I remember wanting to kiss you more than anything in the world. But I never did."

She didn't say anything. She just gazed out the window. I wish I knew what she was thinking at that moment.

"I'll go. I'm sorry for bringing it up. Call me if you need anything." I wanted to leave as fast as possible and keep some of my dignity intact.

"I guess . . . I'm lucky, aren't I?" she whispered.

The Jackets

My hand hovered inches away from the brass doorknob. Wow. That was definitely not the response I was expecting.

"Don't go. Please . . . stay with me," Emma said.

I had never imagined this scenario. I had always thought that she'd give me a tight-lipped smile and say, "Thank you, but I'm in love with _Insert guy's name here_," and I'd be on my way, broken heart in tow. Find a gay bar somewhere, get drunk, sleep with some random woman and move on with my sad, pathetic little life. But this? What just happened? It was a miracle.

"Faith? You okay?"

"I'm perfect."

"Why do you love me? Why do you care about me when I can't even stand the sight of my own face?"

"I don't know. I like the way you look at me. You pay attention to me. You listen to the things I say as though I am the only person in the room. I love the way you try to twist phantom pieces of your hair after you get a haircut. You keep trying to grab at something that's not there. It's adorable." I fidgeted with my fingers.

She picked up her cane. Her knuckles were almost white, she was gripping it so hard. She took a few wobbly steps toward me and stopped when she was face to face with me.

I looked into her hazel eyes. She dropped her wooden cane and embraced me. Emma planted a soft kiss on my cheek and whispered, "I love you, too, Faith."

I wrapped my arms around her and couldn't help but sob as I buried my face in her neck.

Emma . . . always her and no one else.

Yellow

Audrey wallpapered her walls with the love letters Keith had sent her. Lies. Keith was the Prince of Lies. She wept over the latest letter, wondering how she could have possibly believed that he was going to change his bad habits all because she had asked him to. She should have known better. She should have left him when she had the chance. Why didn't she listen to her own advice? It was her heart that confused her. That fist-sized muscle that pumped blood into her body was always willing to give him a second chance.

Keith pounded on the door. "Open the door, Audrey."

She gasped in fear, but nevertheless took his most recent letter and glued it to the one space she had left on the wall.

"If walls had eyes, they would weep at the sight of me," she whispered as she took a step back.

His letters covered the left side of their room. Her legs gave out, and she slid down to the floor. Audrey hugged her knees and softly rocked herself.

"Fall or fly. Fly or die. Fight or die . . . " she muttered to herself.

"Open the door, you worthless bitch. You think you're going to leave? I'll kill you before I let you set foot outside this house," he shouted as he continued banging on the door.

One of the screws flew off the hinge and landed by her feet. She screamed and ran to the window. Her face contorted as she sobbed. It physically hurt to cry. She could feel the blood slowly dripping from the corner of her lips. She could barely keep her left eye open, it was so badly bruised.

I don't want to die.

Audrey opened the window and thought about jumping. She was on the second floor. She wondered if she would land safely. If she broke her leg, she was as good as dead.

God, what should I do?

As a reply, the wind blew into the room and peeled a number of the letters off the wall. They danced and spun around her like a miniature tornado as they made their way to the door. It was as though the letters were offering her protection from the drunken man on the other side of the door. This was the answer to her prayer.

"If walls had eyes, they would weep at the sight of me," Audrey whispered.

She climbed out the window, sat on the sill with her legs dangling and let herself fall to the lawn below. The fall was a lot slower than she had expected. Almost as though someone had slowed the world down and allowed her to have additional time to make her escape. She thought about the darkness she was running from, and, before she knew it, she was on the ground . . . safe. Her bare feet had landed on the emerald-green grass with a soft thud. She hesitated for a moment, allowing herself to look up at the window. The letters fluttered out the window and floated above her head for a moment.

Audrey quickly ran inside the house and grabbed the bags she had packed. They waited for her by the entrance. She picked up her keys and the pale lemon jacket. She heard Keith still struggling with the door upstairs. She didn't waste any more time wondering how long it would take him to burst into the room. She walked out of the house, got in her silver Toyota and drove to the police station.

As soon as Audrey parked the car, she checked her face in the rearview mirror. She cried when she saw the dark purple bruise around her eye. She studied her face and assessed the damage: a bruised bottom lip and a deep cut on her left cheek that was black and blue around the edges. She shuddered as she remembered the hatred on Keith's face as he threw a beer bottle at her.

Audrey dried her eyes and put on a pair of dark sunglasses. When she walked into the police station, she felt the cold marble floor against her dirty feet and realized she had forgotten to put on a pair of shoes. After checking in with a desk sergeant, she sat down and spotted a set of brown footprints she had left on the clean white floor. Audrey felt her face grow warm from embarrassment. While she waited, she tried to pull her jeans down low enough to cover her feet.

When you're running for your life, you shouldn't care if you have shoes on your feet.

"Ma'am, you're next. How can I help you?" said a tiny brunette in a navy blue uniform. She frowned when she saw Audrey without shoes, but asked her to fill out some forms.

Audrey returned to her seat, lowered her head and started writing in the blank spaces of the paperwork. Then she returned the forms to the officer, who wore a silver tag with her name: Alexandra Bradley.

"Okay, what's this about?" Officer Bradley asked without looking at Audrey.

"I need to file a restraining order," Audrey explained as she self-consciously put her hand over her mouth. She wasn't sure whether or not she wanted sympathy.

"Sure. Can you please sign this log and show me your driver's license?"

"Yeah, sure," Audrey replied.

As Audrey signed in, Officer Bradley looked at her closely for the first time. Audrey searched for her wallet in her purse, and as she did her sunglasses slipped down the bridge of her nose, revealing a bruised and cut face to the police officer. Audrey watched as the woman's curt smile vanished. Her mouth hung open for a moment as she studied Audrey's delicate features. Audrey's eyes watered as her vulnerability showed.

"I'll be right back, sweetheart, you just wait here." Officer Bradley turned around and left Audrey all alone at the counter.

Audrey's hands began to tremble, her knees grew weak, she wasn't sure how much longer she would be able to stand on her bare feet. She suppressed the urge to sob, but felt as though her heart was going to explode from all the sadness, anger and pain she carried. Audrey decided that it would be best for her to have a seat and wait for the woman to return.

Impossible.

That's what Audrey thought when she saw a MISSING poster. The girl on the wall had a heart-shaped face, with expressive green eyes, long black hair that grazed her shoulders and thin but shapely lips. She ripped the poster from the wall and held it in her hands. She exhaled all of the air out of her lungs and felt even more alone than she did before.

Penelope.

It was so strange to think of her gone. Such an intelligent, funny and witty young woman . . . gone. According to the information on the poster, Penelope had been missing for the past five days. Audrey couldn't believe it. She had been so out of it that she didn't even know that her friend was lost, possibly dead.

The Jackets

Chills ran up and down her spine. She couldn't explain why she got that feeling. For some reason . . . she knew Penelope was no more.

Audrey took two steps back and tripped on one of the chairs. She felt her body begin to tumble face forward. Before she knew it, she had made up her mind to just let herself fall. *What's one more bruise? Who cares?*

She was already imagining the way her face would hit the white marble floor and all the blood she would spill. The blood would contrast beautifully against the pale white. Then everything came to a stop, and her stomach lurched. She felt a warm, strong hand against her abdomen. Someone caught her. She didn't fall.

"Are you all right?" a man asked, all the while keeping his arm around her waist.

"No," Audrey whispered.

"Here, let me help you get to the chair."

Audrey didn't want to look at him. Just by the sound of his voice, she knew that he was handsome.

Whatever you do . . . don't look at him.

She felt his strong hands releasing their grip on her waist. He helped Audrey sit down on one of the uncomfortable grey plastic chairs. Still . . . she didn't raise her blue eyes to meet his.

"There you go."

Without meaning to, she looked up at him and smiled —he was a policeman. She hissed as she felt the pain on her bottom lip and quickly retracted the facial expression she had given him. She remembered the state she was in and quickly lowered her gaze. The damage was done. He had seen all there was to see.

"He hit me," Audrey said.

She was unable to control a tear sliding down her cheek. Haltingly, Audrey told him what happened to her. She wanted to say it out loud for her own sake, to confirm that this was reality, not a dream. She looked at the cop and waited for him to say something. His face was blank. Yet . . . his black eyes held a fury she had never seen in anyone before.

"He hit me . . . and I don't know why. I would spend days trying to figure out what it was I did to make him do this to me . . . spent hours locked up in my room, with him banging on the door telling me what a worthless bitch I was. All the while I tried to figure out what I could do to make him better. To make him love me, and you know what he did to me whenever I tried? Beat me. Then . . . he'd write love letters saying how sorry he was and how he needed my help in order to change."

As she spoke, her eyes remained glued to the officer's pitch-black gaze. "I wallpapered my wall with all the letters he wrote. I almost went crazy reading them over and over again . . . until I jumped out the window, because that was the only way I could get out of the house. I still don't know why my legs aren't broken."

"When did he do that to you?" the policeman asked, gesturing to her face and then crossing his arms.

"This morning, after I told him I was leaving. God . . . I was so scared; my hands were trembling something awful."

Audrey wrung her hands and laced her fingers together. Her tears continued to fall freely. It was an effortless dance —the water gathering in the corners of her eyes, sliding down her cheeks, hanging delicately from her chin, landing on the palm of her hand, slowly gathering into a miniature pool.

"How many times has he hit you?"

"Many. I never thought I'd allow a man to do this to me. I always told myself that if a man ever laid a finger on me, that'd be the end of it. But for some dumb reason I always managed to forgive him. Well, you know what? This time around I didn't feel so forgiving." Audrey slipped her sunglasses back on.

"Are you here to file a restraining order?"

"Yes."

The Jackets

"Okay. . . . " The officer walked away, leaving Audrey to her thoughts.

She wanted to kick herself. Why was she thinking about jumping into the arms of yet another man?

Haven't I had enough with Keith? Do I want another man to turn me into a punching bag?

"Miss?" Officer Bradley called to her.

Audrey looked up, went up to the counter and took some more forms. She filled everything out that same day. She wanted to move on with her life.

The first couple of weeks after her escape, Audrey did the best she could to reshape her life. She started doing simple things, like waking up early in the morning and having a nice breakfast of waffles and syrup or cereal. She got a job at a local pharmacy developing film. She didn't want to deal with the rumors and sympathetic looks from her old co-workers at the department store she had worked at with Penelope.

Stacie Maxwell, her best friend, let her stay with her until she pulled her life together.

"So what are you going to do today?" Stacie asked as Audrey handed her a cup of coffee.

"Well, I've saved up enough money for a security deposit and the month of rent for an apartment. I think it's time for me to go."

"Are you sure about that? You know you can stay here as long as you need to."

"Thanks for the offer, but I need to do this . . . alone. I don't want to be afraid anymore. I'm tired of feeling like I need to be surrounded by people in order to feel safe," Audrey said.

She picked up the phone and dialed the number for the apartment complex that Stacie had recommended. It rang a few times. She took several deep breaths while she waited for someone to answer. She wanted to be independent. She wanted to depend on her own strength.

"Thank you for calling Sparrow Apartments, this is Linda. How can I help you?" a soft feminine voice said over the phone.

"Hi . . . I'm calling to see if you have any apartments available," Audrey said.

"What size apartment are you looking for?" Linda asked.

"A one bedroom."

"Any pets?"

She heard the movement of a pen scratching over paper. "No."

"How soon do you need an apartment?"

"As soon as possible."

"I have a one bedroom you can move into next week. Is that soon enough for you?"

"Perfect."

"Would you like to stop by, look at the apartment and leave a deposit?"

"Yeah, sure. I'll come by later today."

"I'll be here until five o'clock."

"I'll be there at two-thirty," Audrey said.

"Great. I'll see you then."

"Bye."

Audrey placed the phone back on the cradle and then looked at her friend's kitchen. It was such a bright, happy-looking place. Bright lemon yellow walls—paintings of vibrant vegetables made by her artist friends, wind chimes made out of stained glass, figurines on the windowsill. Audrey surveyed Stacie's kitchen and wished it all for herself. She wanted a peaceful life, too.

"Hi! You must be Audrey," Linda said as she walked up to her with an extended hand.

"Yes," Audrey said as she shook her hand. "How did you know?"

"You said you'd be here at two-thirty and here you are right on time."

Linda gave Audrey a tour of the premises and the apartment she was going to live in. Linda had a wonderful sense of humor. Audrey never remembered her mother being so light-hearted. She couldn't believe that Linda and her mother were the same age.

"It has a new dishwasher and a microwave. Free water and heat. You have access to the swimming pool and the basketball court," Linda enumerated.

"Well, this is a very nice apartment. How much is it a month?" Audrey asked.

"The first two months are half price. Afterwards, it'll be six hundred a month."

"Great. I'll take it. Where do I sign?"

She was excited to be able to cross one thing off her list.

"Oh, my goodness, I can't accept this," Audrey said when Stacie's parents gave her a brand new couch.

"Nonsense. Take it," Elaine, Stacie's mother, said.

Audrey was embarrassed. She knew she should've kept her mouth shut when she told Stacie how much she adored the navy-blue-colored couch she saw in the Ikea catalog.

Audrey bit her bottom lip with excitement, extended her hand, then hesitated and reached out once more, carefully touching the soft fabric. She couldn't contain her happiness any longer and bounced with joy a few times next to the new couch.

"Here's a little something else. Don't worry. This one is not new," Jason, Stacie's father, said.

Audrey had only seen them a few times, and she never knew the extent of their kindness until now. Not one person from her own family had shown up to help her move into her new apartment. Only Stacie and her parents.

"We'll help you put it together," Jason said as he carried in a small dining room set.

"No! Now, this is too much!"

"Think nothing of it," Stacie announced. "You can make it up to us by cooking dinner for us."

"Oh, I'll be happy to!"

Are they paper-doll parents? Audrey asked herself as she watched the Maxwell's interact with each other. *Was I the only one with poor and crazy parents?*

Elaine had salt-and-pepper hair that was styled into a bob. Her skin was tan from their recent cruise vacation to the Caribbean. She was classically beautiful, as was her wardrobe. Audrey thought of her as a brunette Grace Kelly.

Jason, on the other hand, had a head full of powder-white hair, and, like his wife, his skin was tanned from the cruise. He, too, was an elegant dresser. Audrey watched the way he behaved toward his wife, the way he wrapped his arm around her waist, tucked her hair behind her ear with the utmost care and kissed her on the forehead. Audrey smiled and looked away.

"Anyone in the mood for pizza?" Audrey asked.

"I could go for a few slices of pizza," Jason confirmed.

Audrey picked up her cell phone and placed an order for two medium pizzas. She was surprised to hear the variety of toppings everyone wanted. Stacie wanted pineapple and ham on half of the pizza. Elaine wanted broccoli and tomatoes on her half. Jason wanted everything, but all Audrey wanted was plain cheese.

Audrey spent the afternoon with the Maxwell's, putting things away and organizing her new apartment. They turned the radio to the Oldie's station and sang along to the Beatles, the Drifters, the Temptations, the Supremes and the Four Seasons. The only time it got a little awkward was when Elaine suddenly burst into tears.

"Are you all right?" Audrey asked.

"Oh, sweetie, I'm sorry. I promised Stacie that I wouldn't overreact, but seeing your face all roughed up . . . well, it breaks my heart." Elaine turned her gaze toward her husband.

He shook his head and shushed his wife.

"Oh, please don't cry," Audrey whispered.

Audrey started to pick up the empty pizza boxes and the dirty paper plates, mostly because she didn't know what else to do. She didn't know how to comfort Stacie's mother.

"Let me help you," Stacie said as she started picking up some of the used cups and dirty napkins. Both friends walked to the kitchen and threw all of the garbage into a big black trash bag

"WTL," Stacie whispered. It was their code for "We'll Talk Later."

"So . . . what was that all about?" Audrey asked as soon as Stacie's parents had left.

Stacie took a deep breath and sighed until she emptied her lungs.

"Before she married my father, she was married to his best friend before he was drafted for the war. He went crazy during his time in Vietnam. There were moments when he would wake up in the middle of the night and not know who she was. So whenever that happened, he imagined her to be the enemy.

"He thought he was still in the jungle fighting the war. He almost threw her out the window once. The only thing that saved her was Daddy knocking on the door just as he was getting ready to push her out. My dad heard her screaming inside and broke the door down."

"Are you serious?" Audrey asked.

"Yeah."

"That's why she's so upset over my situation. I reminded your mom of all that stuff."

"Exactly."

"I'm sorry. I'm so sorry." Audrey shook her head.

"It's not your fault."

Stacie noticed how sad her friend had become. She tried to cheer her up by asking, "Were you really named after Audrey Hepburn?"

"Yeah. My mom rented *Breakfast at Tiffany's* when she was pregnant with me. I would kick her whenever Audrey Hepburn appeared on the screen. At that time my parents had decided that they were going to name me Emily. But the following week Mom watched *Sabrina* and the same thing happened. As soon as Audrey Hepburn showed up, I would start kicking. She rented Audrey Hepburn movies for about a month, until my parents decided to name me after her."

It was one of the few pleasant memories she had of her mother, even if it was before she was born. It didn't matter. It was something that showed her that she had been loved at some point in her life by her mother.

"How's your mom?" Stacie asked.

"Who knows? Probably with some guy at a bar getting drunk," Audrey mumbled.

"Oh, before I forget. Here." Stacie dug her hand into her pocket and pulled out a little plastic card, "From me to you."

"What's this?"

It was a gift certificate to a nearby supermarket.

"Oh, geez. Will it ever end?" she asked as she looked at how much she had been given.

"You'll need it."

"It's too much."

"That's minimum for an apartment with no food in it. I should know," Stacie argued.

The Jackets

"You're crazy."

"You still need it, and I know all of your money went to the first two months of rent."

"I hate it when you're right. You know that?"

"And I love it when you flare your nose that way."

Stacie tried to mimic her. Audrey giggled. Both friends looked at each other and laughed.

She pulled her pale lemon jacket closer to her body and suppressed the urge to shudder from the cold. She was at the grocery store trying to decide between two different kinds of frozen dinner when she saw him. Her heart skipped a beat. It was the police officer who had caught her at the station. She thought about going up to him to say hello, but she figured that sort of thing happened to him all of the time. He probably didn't even remember her.

Audrey looked in his direction, trying to see what he was buying. She found the perfect opportunity when he left his shopping cart behind and wandered off into the next aisle.

Audrey held back the urge to giggle as she tiptoed her way toward his cart. She stretched her neck and looked at the things he had picked to eat. She remembered that Stacie mentioned that it was the best way to know what kind of a man he was. Doritos, Red Bull, popcorn, bread, canned soup, toilet paper, milk, pasta and spaghetti sauce. He seemed normal enough.

"Hello," he said.

Shit.

She looked up and flashed what she hoped was her best smile.

"Oh, hi," she said feeling her face flush. She thought about walking away, but it didn't look like she was going to have a smooth getaway, so she stayed put.

"Nice to see you again," he said.

"Nice to see you, too. I don't think I ever got your name when we first met . . . or a chance to thank you."

"Colin," he said and extended his hand.

"At least its official this time," she laughed, taking his hand and shaking it warmly. "I'm Audrey."

"So . . . sneaking a peek into my cart, huh? I didn't know women still did that." He grinned.

"Yeah, guilty as charged. Are you going to arrest me?"

"Do you want me to arrest you?" Colin said as he raised an eyebrow.

Oh boy. She didn't know how to answer that. Guys ignoring her she could handle. Guys treating her like crap—she could deal with that, too. But flirting? Niceness? It was all so strange to her.

"It depends," she answered tentatively.

"On what? Will it get me a date?"

"You're pretty forward for a guy who doesn't know anything about me," Audrey said.

"Au contraire, mademoiselle," he said with a fake French accent as he raised his index finger in the air. "You're five-feet-four-inches tall, weigh one hundred and thirty pounds, blue eyes, brown hair, your address listed is 1023 Garfield Lane, but I know you don't live there anymore because that was the house you shared with your ex . . . who FYI . . . got arrested yesterday for disturbing the peace for the tenth time in a row and for being drunk in public. Just in case you wanted to know." He winked.

When she heard about Keith, it was as though she felt all the weight of the world leave her body. Audrey wanted to correct him. She no longer weighed one hundred and thirty pounds. That was her weight from the last time she renewed her license. But that was something she didn't necessarily want to share.

The Jackets

"You were really curious about me, weren't you? I guess it doesn't hurt that you can easily have access to all of that information."

"I'm sorry. The truth is, Alexandra made a copy of your driver's license. I looked at it and memorized the numbers. And about your ex . . . well, let's just say he made it really easy for me to slam his face against the hood of my car when I cuffed him.

"Listen . . . why don't we pay for our groceries, and then let me take you out to dinner or something. We can talk there instead of in the middle of the supermarket," Colin suggested.

She took a deep breath and nodded.

Colin smiled. They got in line at the register and paid for their things. Colin even helped her put her groceries in her trunk.

"Where would you like to eat?" he asked.

"I don't know. What kind of food do you like?"

"Anything that's cooked. Actually, even if it's burnt I don't mind it all that much," Colin replied.

"There's a nice pizza place not too far from here. We could go there if you want."

"Okay. I don't know where it is, so I'm going to have to follow you," he said.

"All right." Audrey got in her car and waited for Colin to get in his car and pull up behind her. He flashed the lights of his blue truck to identify himself.

"Must be you," she whispered to herself.

She pressed the accelerator and headed for the restaurant.

"You have cheese on your chin," Audrey pointed out.

She managed to see the humor in having pizza twice on the same day. Colin ran his hands along his chin and managed to pull a long string of mozzarella off his face.

"So, what have you been up to these past few weeks?"
Colin asked.

"Not much. Trying to regroup, basically to get my life to-gether for once. Small things have become big steps for me. Like getting an apartment, paying my bills, going to work and having lunch with my friends. You know, normal things like that."

"Things people take for granted, you think?"

"Yeah."

"So what do you want to do next?"

"Save money and get a house. Not a big one or anything like that. I'd like a small house, something I can paint any color I want. I don't like the color of my apartment. It's like beige or something. I just don't like it."

"And what colors would you paint the rooms if you could?" Colin asked, taking another bite of his pizza.

"Well, I would paint my bedroom peach, the second bed-room would be sky blue and the kitchen would be cherry red. How original is that? I'm pretty sure there are a lot of house-wives that have a red kitchen with little apple motifs and all that kinda stuff, but that's what I want. The dining room would be pale yellow and the living room . . . I'm not sure what color I would pick for it. Probably more yellow or some-thing like that," Audrey said.

"Nice."

"You think I'm weird, don't you?"

"No, no, it's just that those are interesting colors, that's all."

"Anyway . . . what about you? What's your story? You al-ready know mine."

"What do you want to know?"

"The basics, I guess. I don't know what we should talk about," Audrey confessed.

"Well . . . let's see. I've been a cop for ten years and I love my job. I have a pitbull named Bill. I hate the person in my building, whoever he or she is, that doesn't clean the lint rack in the dryer. Turn ons? Brunettes. Turn offs? Women with high-pitched, squeaky voices. For some reason it makes me think of Minnie Mouse. How's that for a start?"

Audrey smiled, "That's pretty good."

"I hope you don't mind me asking this, but . . . how did you meet your last boyfriend?"

"At a party. We were both kinda drunk. We made out in a closet and were attached to the hip afterwards. No talking involved." She gave him a sad smile.

He reached over the table and touched her hand. Audrey gasped and drew her hand back so fast she knocked down her glass of water.

"I'm sorry." She took a handful of napkins and dabbed the mess away.

"It's okay. I'm the one who should apologize. I should've known better," Colin said as he helped her clean up the spilled water.

Audrey blushed. She touched her warm cheeks. All he did was reach out and touch her hand. Why did that scare her the way it did? Could it have been the electricity that ran through her when their skin made contact?

Audrey wanted to know what he wanted. She wanted to know what he was thinking. Why was he so interested in her? She didn't want to get hurt again. She didn't want to hurt his feelings either if he really was a nice guy. What if he wasn't? This wouldn't be the first time someone acted friendly toward her just to get to her.

"Listen, nothing personal, but you just seem too nice, and I don't know if I can handle that right now. Let me cut through all the crap because I don't need any more grief from another man, okay?" Audrey warned.

"All right, I understand."

Audrey pulled a gun out of her purse. It was a Derringer. His eyes widened with surprise. She definitely had his attention now.

"I have a license for this, in case you're wondering. I know how to use it. I refuse to get hurt in any way. Not by you or any other man out there. If you have a girlfriend or a wife, tell me now. If you have a thing for women you think need to be rescued, let me know that, too. Because, you know what? I don't need to be saved. I saved myself from the biggest fucking scum of the earth. I survived him, I can sure as hell survive you and anything else you've got."

Her breathing quickened. Her chest rose and fell so fast that she thought her lungs were going to burst out of her ribs. She had never spoken like that to anyone. She was excited and scared at the same time.

Colin swallowed the bite of pizza he had been chewing and tried not to choke. He had never been so turned on in his life. The way she talked to him. Here he had thought she was a delicate little thing that needed protection. He was happy she proved him wrong.

"Wow. You're a feisty little thing, aren't you?" He couldn't help but smile.

"I'm serious," she warned.

"Oh, trust me. I'm serious, too," he said lifting his hands in surrender.

"So?"

"I can't force you to trust anything that I say. I can't promise you that everything I say or do will be perfect because, sweetheart, I'm not. I have no intention of being perfect any time soon. What I can tell you is that I'll do my best to make sure you never cry," Colin promised.

Audrey didn't know what to say to that. It was the most honest thing a man had ever said to her.

"What now?" she asked.

"You can start by giving me your phone number," Colin said.

"Okay, and then what?"

"Maybe I'll call you sometime this week."

"And then?"

"I'll ask you out on a proper date . . . at least one where you don't pull your gun out."

"Oh, sorry." She picked up her gun and put it back inside her purse. "Are you going to wait until the end of the date to kiss me?"

"Only if you want me to."

"Okay."

She stood up. Together they cleaned up the table and dumped their dirty plates in the trash bin.

"Don't forget your jacket," Colin reminded Audrey.

"Thanks." She smiled.

"Here, let me help you with that," he said as he held the pale yellow jacket for her and helped her put it on.

"Are you always this nice?"

"No. Not really. Guys don't usually help each other put clothes on," he joked.

"You know what I mean."

Audrey couldn't help but smile. The ivory satin lining in her jacket caressed her skin as she slipped it on. It made her feel safe and happy, as if good things could actually happen to her.

"You know something?"

"Tell me," Audrey said.

"You look good in that."

"Thank you. It's my lucky jacket."

Navy

His green eyes searched for her face in the crowd. She wasn't his to claim, probably never would be. He caught a glimpse of her brown hair before he saw her face.

"Clara," he shouted.

"Excuse me," he mumbled as he made his way through a sea of people.

"Jack?" She tilted her head toward the sound of his voice. But she couldn't pinpoint exactly where he was.

Jack could see her profile.

He called her name once more. She smiled and waved at him excitedly when she spotted him in the middle of the crowd. His heart stopped when he saw the look on her face, and he made himself take a deep breath before he took a step toward her.

Jack had to remind himself that no matter how he felt . . . she was his brother's wife. And he was standing in for Jeremy, only because his brother could not make it to the airport on time.

"Hey, Jack," Clara said as she put her luggage on the ground and gave him a warm hug.

He let his hands hover awkwardly behind her back for a moment until he finally decided to hug her back. He took a deep breath and smelled her hair. She smelled like shampoo and tangerines. He didn't mean to, but he held her for a while longer than he should have.

"How was your trip?" Jack asked as he picked up one of her suitcases.

"It sucked. I spent four hundred dollars to earn twenty-four dollars and ninety-five cents. Can you believe that?" She rolled her eyes and picked up the smaller suitcase.

"At least the food was good."

"What can I say?" he said as he shrugged his shoulders and tried to give her a reassuring smile.

"Anyway, what did I miss while I was away?" she asked as they walked out of the airport.

"Well . . . C.C. almost set the kitchen on fire for the third time since she moved into her apartment. David got dumped yesterday. He's depressed . . . so beware. Umm, let me see. . . . What else did you miss? Jeremy got back from his trip two nights ago, but he's been kinda moody lately."

"Moody? About?"

"I don't know," Jack lied.

Jack knew why his brother was upset. He recently admitted that he had been having second thoughts about his marriage to Clara, that boredom had set in and that he was attracted to other women.

"Jack? Do you know something I don't?" Clara asked as she put her hand on his shoulder.

"Why don't you ask him if there's something bothering him? Okay?"

Clara looked into his eyes to see if she could decipher anything.

On the ride home, they said little to each other, except when they both reached for the knob to change the radio station at the same time. Jack felt what he could only describe as an electric charge when his skin came into contact with

Clara's. He was surprised to see her blush a little as she withdrew her hand from the radio.

"Sorry," he mumbled.

"No, that's okay. I just wanted to listen to something with a little more . . . rock."

"That's cool. Go ahead and change the station."

"Thanks." She turned the silver knob for a few minutes until she stopped at a song she liked. Jack was surprised to hear "Bohemian Rhapsody" by Queen.

"*Mama . . . just killed a man,*" Clara sang along. Jack couldn't help but smile at her impersonation of Freddie Mercury. He found himself humming along until he eventually started singing with Clara . . . loudly. When the slow song changed to a faster tempo, they threw their heads back and forth.

"*So you think you can stone me and spit in my eye,*" Clara sang into an imaginary microphone.

"*So you think you can love me and leave me to die,*" Jack sang into Clara's imaginary microphone. They finished singing the song and laughed.

"I hope you never have to quit your day job," Clara teased.

Jack grinned and shook his head, partly because he had no comeback for her comment and also because he knew he was a terrible singer.

After depositing her bags in the entry hall, Jack was about to take leave, when Clara grabbed his arm.

"Jack?"

"Yeah?" he asked, turning back to her.

"Are you sure there's nothing else you want to tell me about Jeremy before I go up and look for him?"

Jack wanted to tell her, wanted any excuse he could think of to get Clara to break things off with his brother. But no matter how he felt about her, he would never be able to do that. Nothing changed the fact that she was his brother's wife.

"No, nothing," he said, looking straight into her hazel eyes. Clara could tell he was covering something up. Was it that Jeremy was cheating on her? There were no telltale signs, no proverbial lipstick on his collar, no bite marks on his neck or anywhere else on his body. But more often than not, he'd come home with a woman's faint perfume on his clothes and a smug look on his face.

"Okay." She turned away from Jack and headed in to look for her husband.

"Hey, Clara," Jeremy shouted when he heard his wife coming up the stairs.

"Hey," she echoed with a sigh.

"You all right?" he asked with a deep frown.

"Just . . . ," she yawned, " . . . tired."

"What would you like for dinner?" Jeremy asked.

"I don't know . . . wanna order some Chinese food?" Clara called out as she went into their bedroom and flopped on the bed.

"Sounds good. What do you want?"

Jeremy went downstairs to the kitchen. He picked up his cell phone and dialed the number he knew by heart for the restaurant. He grabbed the menu that was pinned on the re-frigerator door.

"What do you want, hon?"

"Sweet and Sour Chicken Combo," she called down.

"Okay," he said. "Hi! I'd like to place an order for delivery."

Clara listened to Jeremy's voice closely, trying to hear a clue, a hint, something that would tell her what it was Jeremy did or didn't do in Chicago. Jack's warning continued to echo in her mind.

Jeremy came up and sat on the bed next to Clara. He put his arm around her like he always did. They were silent for a while, both of them slightly uncomfortable. Jeremy broke the silence.

"So . . . how was your trip?"

The Jackets

She was relieved to have something to talk about. "Well, Florida was interesting, to say the least," Clara began. "I had one woman stop in front of my table and look at my book. I thought she was going to buy it, but she put it down and walked away before I could tell her what the book was about."

"How many copies total?" Jeremy asked.

"One."

"One?"

"One," she repeated dryly.

"Damn."

"I know."

"It's a good book."

"Thanks." She got up from the bed.

"I mean it."

"I know you do," Clara said as she headed for the bathroom.

"Shower?"

"Yeah."

"Okay. I'll let you know when the food gets here," he said.

"Thanks." She closed the bathroom door behind her and turned on the shower. She removed her clothes and stepped into the tub.

Clara tried not to cry as the hot water hit her face. She wasn't sure what to believe now that Jeremy was acting like his normal self. Sometimes she was too scared to come home for fear of what Jeremy she would find. Sweet? Depressed? Arrogant? Which one? It was almost as though he had multiple personalities. She felt lucky that he was never violent toward her in any way. But sometimes she wondered if it were better to have scars and bruises to show the world actual proof of her pain and sorrow.

Clara grabbed the shampoo bottle, poured some of its contents into the palm of her hand and washed her hair. She took a deep breath and let the smell of tangerine and ginger soothe her nerves. By the time she got out of the shower, she didn't know how much of the water pooled at her feet was shower water or tears.

Clara dried off with a navy blue towel. She put on a big white T-shirt and her black pajama bottoms and headed downstairs to wait for their dinner to be delivered.

"You smell nice," Jeremy said.

"Thanks." She sat down, grabbed the remote and turned on the TV. Switching channels mindlessly, she thought about the questions she wanted to ask Jeremy.

Clara tossed the remote aside and asked, "So what about you? How was Chicago?"

Clara's eyes stayed glued to the TV. She watched as a lioness crouched down on the ground, using the brown branches of the bushes to hide herself from her prey. From the corner of her eye, she studied her husband's reaction to her question.

"Nothing exciting . . . really. Meetings, meetings and more meetings."

The lioness was now slowly making her way toward the wildebeest, stopping only when she noticed it flinch.

"Oh? No parties? Nothing like that? Every time you go somewhere, you somehow end up at a party," she said, trying to sound innocent.

"Nope. Just went straight to bed . . . missing you," he added.

The wildebeest escaped, but the lioness now had a better idea on how to catch him next time.

"Hmmm."

There was a knock at the door.

"Ah! Must be our food. I'll get it," Jeremy said a little too enthusiastically.

He ran to the door, leaving her sitting in the living room, watching the unfulfilled lioness trotting away from an unsuccessful hunt.

The Jackets

That night Jeremy fucked her. At least that's what she'd been calling it lately. He stopped making love to her three years ago. She could almost sense him pretending she was someone else whenever he climbed on top of her.

She decided that she would do the same thing.

Clara fantasized about Jack whenever she had to get fucked by Jeremy. She wondered what it would be like to be touched by him. She imagined him kissing her. She thought about the things he might whisper in her ear while they made love. Just thinking about it made her groin tighten.

"Oh, yeah," Jeremy moaned.

Jack.

She climaxed. All the while she whispered his name in her mind over and over again.

"Clara . . . there's something I've been meaning to tell you for the longest time. I don't even know how it happened. It just did," Jack said.

Clara looked radiant. The sun shone on her face, making her skin glow. Her eyes shimmered. He wasn't sure what they looked like more . . . a river of melted bronze or dark honey lit from the inside out.

"Jack . . . " she started to say.

Beep, beep, beep. Jack opened his eyes and stared at the ceiling. Another Clara dream. He rubbed the sand from the corners of his eyes and pushed the button on the alarm clock to silence it.

Half asleep, he made his way to the bathroom. He grabbed his blue toothbrush, put the toothpaste on it and brushed his teeth. As he got ready to spit the foam out of his mouth, the phone rang.

Who would call him so early in the morning? He looked at the green digital numbers on his clock and they flashed seven-ten. He spit the toothpaste foam out of his mouth and rinsed his toothbrush before picking up the phone.

"Hello?" he mumbled as he wiped his lips with the back of his hand.

"Jack?"

His heart stopped beating for a few seconds.

"Hellooo? Jack, are you there?" Clara asked when she didn't hear him reply.

"Yeah. Yeah, I'm here," he said, forcing himself to speak.

"It's Clara."

"I know. . . . "

"Listen, I'm really sorry to call you so early, but I need to talk to you."

"Okay." He sat down and prepared his ear for however long this conversation was going to take.

"But not on the phone," she said.

He stood up and felt relieved that she wanted to talk to him in person. "Right," he said.

"What are you doing after work?"

"Nothing, really. I get out at four. I can meet you wherever you want, at four-thirty if you like."

"Okay, how about the coffee shop by your house?"

"Sounds good to me. I'll see you then."

"Okay, thanks, bye."

"Bye."

Jack waited until she hung up. He heard the soft click of her placing the phone back on its cradle but kept the phone pressed to his ear until it started beeping.

The entire morning was a blur to Jack. He wrote an article for the magazine and answered phone calls. He accepted the fact that he went somewhere inside his brain and pushed a big red button that had AUTOPILOT written on it. He flew under everyone's radar for the entire day. He was thankful for that small miracle because on a normal day, his boss would've been asking him twenty questions about what he was up to.

He waited patiently for four o'clock to come, but at three fifty-eight, he grabbed his keys and his wallet. At three fifty-nine, he was in the elevator, and at four on the dot he was in his hunter-green Jeep leaving the parking lot.

Jack arrived at the café in fifteen minutes and parked in front. Jack sat in his car. He turned the radio on and waited for Clara. He was pretty sure what it was she wanted to talk about.

Five minutes later, Clara's silver Jetta parked right next to him. She didn't notice him. Jack didn't do anything. He didn't blink. He just looked at her. Clara had her sunglasses on. He couldn't help but notice the way her lips were trembling. The ghost of a smile she always had was gone.

He was about to get out of the car when he saw Clara put her head in her hands and cry. The weight of her tears must've been too great for her hands to carry because they slid from her face down to her sides. She sobbed a few times and then rested her forehead on the steering wheel.

He got out of the car and knocked on Clara's passenger-side window. She didn't even lift her head. She rolled her head to the side to see who it was. When Clara saw Jack, she tried to smile for him, but she may as well have kept the same look on her face. She pushed the UNLOCK button. When he heard the locks pop, he opened the door. He sat down beside her and waited for her to say something.

"Hi," she whispered after what seemed like an eternity.

"Hi."

"Why does he hurt me?"

"Jeremy?"

"Yeah."

"Does he . . . " he took a deep breath and tried again, "Does he hit you?"

He shifted uneasily on his seat, waiting for the answer. That, he wouldn't have tolerated at all. Not even from his own brother.

"You know, sometimes I wish he would. It would make it easier for me to leave him."

"So he doesn't hit you."

"No, he doesn't."

"Clara . . . what's this all about? Why did you want to see me?"

"What happened in Chicago?"

"I don't think I'm the right person to tell you this."

"Jack, if you don't tell me, I'll leave him." She pressed her palm against her forehead and shook her head. "If you don't tell me, I'm going to leave him anyway. I just want to know the truth before I go."

"Jesus, Clara!"

He suddenly felt bad for his brother.

"Tell me what happened, Jack," Clara pleaded.

Jack looked into her eyes and found a great sadness hidden deep within them. He had a feeling he would regret his decision, but he wanted to take away that look in her eyes.

"Technically," he started, "nothing happened. But it was something that he wasn't happy about. He wanted to mess around, but he kept reminding himself that he was a married man. He didn't like the fact that he was tied down to you."

With every word he said, he saw Clara's face change from sadness to anger. Her face grew bright pink, and she screamed as she punched and tried to rip the steering wheel out of its place.

"Stupid fucker!" she shouted every time her fist met the steering wheel. She began sobbing uncontrollably and then started gasping for air. Jack held her in his arms and tried to console her as best as he could.

"Breathe, Clara, breathe," he coaxed.

She nodded and took quick short breaths. She put her head on his lap and for a while laid there and tried to catch her breath. Jack ran his fingers through her hair. This was the first time he'd touched her without it being a friendly hug or a quick peck on the cheek.

"I'm so sorry."

"Why?"

"I didn't tell you sooner."

Clara put her fingers on his lips. That silenced everything else he wanted to say.

"Jack, none of this is your fault." She pulled herself away from him and sat up. "This has been something that's been waiting to happen since the day we got married."

"What do you mean?"

"I always suspected that he liked to play around. I thought that if I married him, he would settle down and realize that life with me could still be enough." She shook her head. "I was a fool."

"You were in love. Jeremy's not a bad person. He's just . . . stupid. Jeremy's stupid for making it easy to lose you." He had searched for the right words. He glanced at Clara, he realized even her sadness didn't mask any of her beauty.

"Can you lose something that was never yours to start with?" She pulled out a piece of paper from her jean pocket and handed it to Jack.

He took it from her and unfolded it. It had a woman's name and phone number scribbled on it. *Jessica Sherwood.* The woman who gave this to Jeremy even thought it appropriate to place a little heart above the *i*.

"God, look at this. How fucking high school can you be?"

He handed the paper back to Clara.

She managed to give him the tiniest of smiles.

"Come on, let me buy you a cup of coffee or something," he said.

"I don't know . . . "

"Come on, do you really want to go home?"

Clara shook her head. She took a deep breath and checked her face in the mirror. "I look terrible." She laughed.

"You look great, as always."

"Now I know you're lying."

They both laughed and went into the coffee shop.

"What would you like?" he asked.

Clara looked at the menu for a few seconds and ordered hot chocolate.

"Anything to eat?" Jack asked.

"An everything bagel with cream cheese."

Jack placed the order with the barista.

"I'll have a small cup of coffee and a plain bagel with grape jelly," he said.

"Interesting," she said.

"How so?"

"It's nothing. Just something I say when I don't have anything to add to a conversation."

They sat down and chatted about everything they could think of. Memories, people they thought they knew, the present and their thoughts on what they wanted in the future. Jack made Clara laugh with his best jokes. He was sure that people could hear her laughter a mile away. The only topic they avoided talking about was Jeremy.

"What time is it?" Clara asked.

Jack looked at his watch and said, "Quarter after six."

Clara sighed and grabbed her things.

Jack took out a few dollar bills, left it on the table under his mug and followed Clara as she walked outside.

"I had a nice time, Jack. Thank you for tonight," Clara said.

"You're welcome, I had a lot of fun, too."

Clara looked up at the sky. It was twilight. The stars were starting to come out.

"The stars are beautiful, aren't they?" she whispered sadly.

The Jackets

She turned her gaze toward Jack. He didn't answer her question. They both stood there looking at each other. He nodded. He had no words left in him.

Clara smiled and said, "Good night, Jack."

She leaned forward and hugged him. He felt her heart beating against his chest. Clara pulled herself away. He slipped a hand behind her neck and kissed her. She let out a short gasp, mostly because he surprised her. He felt her body stiffen, but it quickly relaxed as she let herself go. She gave in to the moment.

He gently pushed his tongue inside her mouth. He tasted the chocolate she recently had. Then their lips parted. Almost like waiting for the smoke to clear, he waited to see what she would say or do. He didn't know if she was going to slap him or kiss him back.

"Oh, God," Clara said, her hands covering her face and then just her lips. She started shaking. Her brown hair trembled above her shoulders. She had just kissed her husband's brother. No matter how much she had fantasized about it, this wasn't something that she should've done.

"Clara . . . " he said her name as though it were a prayer.

"I have to go." She got in her car and drove away.

Jack growled in frustration and shouted, "I'm sorry!"

At almost every stoplight, he banged his head against the steering wheel

Stupid, stupid, stupid. I shouldn't have kissed her.

He finally arrived at his house.

"Huh?" He frowned.

Clara's car was parked at the curb.

"Oh, boy," he whispered to himself.

She was sitting on the front steps of his house.

"Clara? What are you doing here?"

She didn't say anything. Calmly she took out a tissue and blew her nose. "Do you ever wish you smoked? Sometimes I do. I could use a cigarette right about now," she finally said.

"What happened?"

She chuckled and said, "I was gonna go home after I ran away from you. Then I realized that I didn't want to. Because in reality, it's just a building I share with another stranger. Two people living in a house together doesn't make it a home. A home is supposed to be a place that's filled with love.

"So halfway to this building I share with my 'husband'," she made quotation marks with her hands, "I was thinking about working things out with Jeremy and avoiding becoming another statistic and all that crap. But . . . I made a U-turn. My hands took over and brought me here."

"I see."

"I sat here wondering how the hell did I end up married to the wrong guy? The wrong brother, for that matter. Why didn't I wait a little longer? You kissed me . . . "

"Clara, I'm sorry about all of this. I should've just kept my big mouth shut. I just . . . I just hated seeing you sad. I hate Jeremy for trying to make a fool out of you."

"I wanted you to kiss me. Sometimes I wonder if I make things happen, know what I mean? I think about you all the time, Jack."

"I've been in love with you since the moment we met. I almost killed myself when Jeremy announced your engagement. I tried to let you go. It almost drove me crazy to do it, but I tried. I went out with other women. But nothing worked."

"Oh, Jack." She stood on the tips of her toes and kissed him.

She caught him by surprise. He scooped her up in his arms and carried her inside the house. He wasn't sure he wanted to think about what he was doing. Nothing, not even his own conscience, could tear him away from her now.

The Jackets

The phone woke him up. Jack rubbed his eyes and then reached for the receiver. It fell on the floor. He mumbled and picked it up.

He pressed the receiver against his ear and said, "Hello?"

"Jack!" It was Jeremy.

His eyes grew wide.

Hearing his brother's voice cleared his mind. He was suddenly wide awake.

"Yeah," he said, trying to sound as normal as possible.

"Have you seen Clara? She never came home last night. I called her cell phone a hundred times, and she never picked up. Do you have any idea where she might be?"

"I saw her yesterday when I got off work, but she said she was going to go straight home." It was half the truth.

"You saw her? Why?"

"She wanted to meet me for coffee. It wouldn't be the first time," Jack said.

"Oh . . . right."

"Sorry I can't help you out."

"That's okay. Give me a call if you hear from her, okay?"

"Sure thing, man."

"Okay, bye."

Jack hung up. He let out a long sigh and looked on the other side of the bed.

"Good morning," she said.

"'morning."

She smiled and stretched.

"Who was it on the phone?"

"Jeremy."

"Uh oh. Is he looking for me?"

"Yep."

"That's my cue." She got out of bed.

She didn't bother to cover herself up. Clara walked to the bathroom and closed the door behind her.

"Well, at least I know she's not shy," Jack whispered to himself.

He heard the toilet flush and shortly afterwards heard the soft motion of a toothbrush. A few minutes later, she stepped out of the bathroom. He was happy to see that she was still naked. He forced himself to look the other way.

"You already saw me naked last night. No need to act shy about it. By the way, I took the liberty of using your toothbrush."

"Sorry, it's just . . . "

"Strange?"

"Not really. Just a little awkward," he admitted.

"Yeah." She picked up her purple underwear from the floor and slipped them on.

"You're leaving?" he asked as she pulled her black T-shirt over her head.

"Gotta go home. I have to talk to Jeremy and end this."

"Are you going to tell him about last night?"

"Are you insane? No, of course not. Unless you have a death wish or something." Clara got on her knees and searched for her jeans.

"There they are," she said as she pulled the jeans from under his bed. She slipped them on.

"Glad to see we're both on the same page," Jack said, a little relieved that he'd be able to live to see another day.

"I don't even like sleeping in the same bed with him. You know . . . there's a difference between making love and being fucked," Clara muttered as she tied the laces on her right sneaker.

"I didn't know things were that bad between you two."

"I don't always tell you everything, Jack." She scanned his room for her missing sneaker.

"I see," he said as he got out of bed and handed her the missing shoe. "Here you go, Cinderella."

"Thanks." She smiled.

The Jackets

"Allow me." Jack got on one knee and slipped the shoe on her foot.

"My naked prince," she mused. "I think I could get used to this."

"Really funny." Jack blushed a little and decided that it would be best if he put some clothes on.

"I have to go."

"It's not midnight yet," he said as he pulled her against him and kissed her.

"I'll be back before you know it."

"All right, call me if things get out of hand," Jack said as he sat down on the corner of the bed.

"I will." She climbed on top of the bed, swiveled in front of him and wrapped her legs around his waist.

The button of her jeans felt cold against his stomach. It soon warmed up. They kissed passionately, tongues dancing slowly inside each others' mouths. Clara giggled and climbed off him. By the time they pulled their lips away, Jack had her jean button and part of her zipper lightly marked on his skin.

"I'll see you later," she said.

"Later," he echoed.

Jack got dressed, ate cereal and watched TV for an hour . . . or more accurately, he switched channels for an hour. He couldn't concentrate on the television; he was so worried about Clara. He wanted to call her and make sure she was okay, but he didn't want to get in the middle of whatever was happening between her and Jeremy. He finally picked up the phone and dialed the first three digits of her cell phone number. He growled in frustration and pressed the red off button.

Two hours passed and still nothing. He was pacing back and forth, from one end of the living room to the other.

"Call me, Clara. Call me and let me know you're okay," he mumbled as he clutched the phone.

He wasn't sure that Jeremy wouldn't hurt her if she tried to leave him. He realized just how little he knew his brother. He wanted to believe that he wouldn't. But when someone is angry, there is no knowing how he or she may react. The thought of something happening to Clara made him crazy.

He started having negative images of Clara and Jeremy having an argument. He continued pacing as he imagined the argument escalating.

Fuck it.

He grabbed his wallet and keys. He drove down to his brother's house at neck-breaking speed.

His tires came to a screeching halt. He was relieved to see that Clara's car was parked in the driveway. He ran to the front door and pounded his fist against it. Jack waited. He let out a sigh of relief when he heard footsteps getting closer to the door. His heart stopped when he saw that it was Clara who opened the door. Jack pulled her into a hug and found it hard to let go of her.

"Jack? Are you okay?" she asked, holding on to him.

"I am now. You?"

"Yeah, I decided to stick around and pack a few things."

"I see."

"Were you worried?"

"Yeah," he admitted.

"I'm sorry. I should've called you."

"Do you need help with anything?"

"Yeah, sure," she said. "My parents will be stopping by in a little bit."

"Cool."

He walked inside, and he could already feel the change the house had undergone. The energy was different. Jack remembered, whenever he visited, there was a neutral feeling to the house. Now? It was filled with sadness, regret and anger. He followed Clara upstairs.

"Hey, Jack," he heard his brother's voice behind him when Jack reached the top of the steps.

He turned around and found Jeremy staring up at him from the bottom of the stairs. There was darkness in his eyes, something that had never been there before.

"Hey, Jeremy," he said, trying to sound as normal as possible.

"Did she ask you to meet here?"

"Yeah," Jack lied.

"So you know then?"

"Yeah, she told me last night. I'm really sorry." He was surprised to find out that there was truth in what he said.

"Did you tell her?" Jeremy asked, his eyes growing darker with anger.

"She found that woman's number all by herself. I had nothing to do with that. You didn't even tell me she gave you her phone number. I told her the rest because she asked me, and I didn't feel like lying to her anymore. She doesn't deserve it. But look at it this way . . . now you're free to screw anyone you want."

"You told her. I know you did." He pointed an accusatory finger at him.

"I didn't say anything," Jack said as he went downstairs and faced his brother.

"You fucking asshole. You're a liar." Jeremy lunged forward, grabbed Jack's shirt and slammed him against the wall.

Jack groaned as the back of his head connected with the brick wall. He literally saw stars.

They pushed and pulled each other into the living room.

"What the hell is going on down there?" Clara called out from upstairs.

"What the fuck is your problem? You don't love her anymore!" Jack said.

"That doesn't mean that I want *you* to have her. I've seen the way you look at her. I'm not blind."

Time almost stopped moving for Jack. He could hear his heartbeat quicken. He took a deep breath and lowered his head. He thought he had kept his feelings hidden. He lifted his gaze just in time to feel Jeremy's fist connect with his jaw. Jack fell back, his head throbbing with pain.

"What's going on in here?" Clara asked as she ran down the stairs.

She saw Jack sprawled on the floor with a bloodied lip. She crouched down and turned her sights on her husband.

"I don't get you," she said. "You ignore me most of the time. You cheat on me at the drop of a hat. You come home smelling like other women. Now you're angry because your brother paid attention to me? And I'm supposed to believe that you give a shit because I'm leaving? Fuck you."

"Clara, I'm sorry. It was never my intention to hurt you. I do love you," he said.

"The road to hell is paved with good intentions. Get out," she said as she ran to the door and opened it.

"I really am sorry." Jeremy grabbed his keys and wallet from the table in the living room.

"Me, too, but I can't do this anymore. I can't be your wife when you don't want me."

Jeremy walked out and closed the door behind him.

"Come on, Jack. Let me put some ice on your jaw." She extended her hand out to him.

Jack took her hand and let Clara help him up. He moved his jaw left and right. He felt a soft pop as though something had fallen back into place.

"Does it hurt?"

"Well, it doesn't make me think of toasted marshmallows, if that's what you mean."

She chuckled and pulled an ice pack out of the freezer. She carefully pressed it against his jaw, which was already starting to swell.

"I'm sorry," she whispered.

"Not your fault."

"He's your brother."

"He'll get over it." Jack hoped what he said was true. He didn't want to think about what the rest of his life was going to be like without his older brother.

Clara moved around the kitchen and poured water into a green teapot. She smiled at Jack and asked him if he would like a cup of tea. He nodded.

"You look like you got in a fight with a gorilla . . . and lost," Joan said.

"Mom, you're not making him feel any better," Clara scolded.

"I'm just being honest," her mother replied.

"Thanks, Mrs. Rose," Jack said.

"Please, call me Joan. Fifty years old and I still can't get used to being a Mrs."

Jack smiled and winced. He had forgotten about his jaw.

"Any other boxes?" Malcolm, Clara's father, asked as he stepped into the kitchen. He adjusted his glasses and waited for a response.

"Nope. Just some clothes and that's it. But I can put that in the car," Clara said.

"Okay. Well, we're gonna go home and put your things in your old room," Malcolm said.

"Sounds like a plan," she said.

"Are you going to come over for dinner?" Joan asked.

"I don't know. Jack, what do you think?" Clara asked.

"What's for dinner?" he asked.

"Food," Joan replied.

Jack nodded and said, "Food sounds . . . good."

"Great, we'll see you at six-thirty," Joan said.

Clara walked her parents to the door and kissed them goodbye.

"They're cool," Jack said.

"Yeah."

"What's the matter?"

"There's something I want to show you."

"Okay." He followed her upstairs.

Jack walked into the bedroom she had shared with Jeremy. There was nothing of Clara's left in the room. The only thing that would've let anyone know that a woman had lived there was a little night table on the left side of the bed with romance novels and some makeup on top. That was it.

"Everything all right?" Clara asked.

"Things have moved really fast."

"I'm really sorry I got you mixed up in this mess."

Clara pulled out a white box from deep inside the closet. She sat on the corner of the bed and placed it on her lap.

"What is it?"

"You don't remember?"

She pulled the lid off and carefully peeled away the tissue paper that protected what was inside.

"You gave me this for my birthday three years ago. Remember? It was during a week that Jeremy was away on a business trip. I think he was in Miami or California."

"Oh, yeah."

Clara took out the navy-colored jacket that was inside the white cardboard box. It was a Chinese jacket with gold dragons and good-luck flowers stitched on the navy-colored satin. Jack had bought it for her because she noticed that the jean jacket she wore had a tear on the shoulder. It was something so small that no one else would have noticed. But he didn't

The Jackets

want to see her walking around like that, so he bought the jacket for her.

"I've never worn this," she confessed.

"How come?"

"It made me sad."

"Really? Why?"

"Jeremy sent me roses and balloons from wherever the hell he was. But you know something?"

"Tell me."

"I didn't care for any of it. You, on the other hand, gave me this jacket. I knew you thought about every single detail in it. I knew you noticed the tiny tear I had in my jean jacket. I loved the fact that you thought about getting this for me. That meant more to me than all the flowers and balloons in the world." She smiled.

"I really wished it had been more. I thought you hated it since you didn't wear it."

"It made me sad. This was what made me realize that I may have married the wrong brother." She started to cry.

"Don't," he whispered as he wiped her tears away.

"I'm sorry. I wish . . . ," she sighed, "things had been different for us. Know what I mean?"

Jack nodded.

"Ready?" she asked.

"Yeah, let's go eat some food."

"Are you going to be able to eat with your jaw all messed up?"

"It's not that bad. It looks worse than it really is," he replied.

Clara took the midnight blue jacket out of the box and slipped it on. Jack was happy to see that it fit her perfectly.